CLUES

Across

25. She was in _____ Heaven
33. Mean utterance

Down

16. The Taming of ___ Shrew

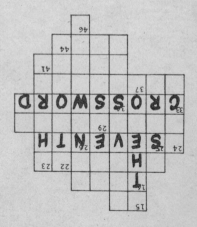

Also by Herbert Resnicow
Published by Ballantine Books

MURDER ACROSS AND DOWN

THE SEVENTH CROSSWORD

Herbert Resnicow

Puzzles by Henry Hook

BALLANTINE BOOKS • NEW YORK

Library of Congress Catalog Card Number: 85-90750

ISBN 0-345- 32732-2

Manufactured in the United States of America

First Edition: October 1985

To Carolyn Penzler who opened the door for me

 **1**

"**H**OW CAN THERE BE SEVEN PUZZLES," KAREN KARAS asked, her big dark eyes questioning each of her colleagues in turn, "when there are only six of us?" Her short black hair, tailored tweed pantsuit, and low heels did their best to make her look like the popular conception of a professor, but even a suit of armor could not have concealed her beauty.

Her five associates were seated in the empty classroom in student chairs arrayed in a semi-circle around Karen's desk. Professor Dag Norstad, wearing his usual vested suit although the weather was warming, looked nearsightedly over his wire-rimmed glasses as he asked, "Are you sure, Dr. Karas? It is highly improbable that this is so."

"Impossible, you mean," Professor Bruce Yablonski said, a grin on his chubby face. "You statisticians would say it's highly probable the sun will rise tomorrow."

"It is by no means certain, Dr. Yablonski," Dag said.

"Let me see that puzzle," Professor Carl Richter asked, extricating his huge bulk from the student chair and heaving toward Karen's desk.

Karen pushed aside her open attaché case and spread

out the collated piles of crossword puzzles. "Here are the filled-out crosswords we constructed. Six. Here are the sets of blanks and clues for us to use in solving one another's puzzles. And here is the seventh puzzle. Unsolved. One copy only. No signature or code number."

Carl Richter picked up the seventh crossword. "It looks just like the others, fifteen by fifteen, standard type, all letters crossed. Word length seems about average too. Could be one of ours at first glance."

"There's a cryptic clue"—Dag Norstad had gotten up and was looking around Carl's arm—"at 15 Across, 'preventive measure?' The set we constructed for today was to have only standard dictionary definitions."

"It's got to be for Humboldt." Professor Jennifer Zapata squeezed her skinny little body fiercely between Carl and Dag. "Somebody's trying to tell the Grand Duke to do a little horsework too, that it's not just for us peasants."

"Who has time to play games like that?" Bruce Yablonski asked. "I'm lucky to get six hours' sleep a night."

"Maybe you should spend less time brown-nosing your tenure committee," Jennifer Zapata said. "The three of you"—her wave took in Karen and Dag too—"are slaves to the system."

"If you were up for tenure in the English department," Karen said, "where there are ten applicants for each job—"

"And if the alternative was to be an actuary for some big insurance company—" Dag Norstad said.

"Or had four kids to support," Bruce Yablonski said, "and there are hundreds of Ph.D.'s in psychology driving cabs—"

"Let's see how you act, Zapata," Professor Evelyn Tinguely said, pushing her long golden hair from her face, "next year when *you're* up for tenure."

"At least I won't get it on my back," Jennifer said.

"I'm certain of that," Evelyn murmured sweetly.

Carl Richter stepped between them as Jennifer started to go for her blond tormentor. Frustrated, Jennifer yelled, "You're a disgrace to the Movement, Tinguely. You take all the benefits I demonstrated for and then sell out."

"Shut up, Jenny." Karen slammed her hand down hard on the desk. "You started it with your crack about Bruce. Do you think it's fun not knowing, after six years of teaching, if you have a job or not? Not knowing if you can buy a house or have a child?"

"You sold out too, Karas," Jenny sneered. "You and that wimpy husband of yours won't lift a finger to get your rights."

"I just hope I'm around next year, Zapata," Karen said. "I'm going to *volunteer* to be on your tenure committee."

"They can't turn me down," Jenny retorted. "I'm the only Hispanic woman on this whole lily-white campus. They even *dream* of refusing me tenure, I'll shut the whole place down."

"That threat isn't going to work forever," Carl Richter said. "You haven't published a damn thing worthwhile since you got your doctorate. Isabel Macintosh is dean of faculty now, and she doesn't take shit from anybody."

"Can we not get back to the seventh crossword, please?" Dag Norstad asked, and turned to Carl. "Was that one in with the others?"

"It had to be, Dag; I just picked up whatever was in the Project's pigeonhole."

"That pigeonhole is unlabeled," Bruce Yablonski pointed out. "How would any outsider know about the Project or where to put things?"

"Everyone," Evelyn said, "especially the other members of the Crossword Club, knows we're doing *something* with crosswords."

"But only *we* know the details," Bruce insisted. "This puzzle is the right size and type in every way."

"Are you saying that one of us constructed an extra puzzle?" Evelyn asked. "Whatever for? Even if I had the time, I wouldn't waste it on making extra puzzles. Three a week is plenty."

"Who gives a damn if anyone slipped in an extra puzzle?" Jennifer asked. "Throw it away if it bothers you, Karas."

"I can't do that," Karen said. "Professor Humboldt might have constructed it himself."

"That is not very probable." Dag's gray eyes looked puzzled. "Why should the professor, who has led the group with impeccable rigor until now, suddenly introduce a wild card?"

"Spoken like a true mathematician," Bruce said, smiling. "But as a psychologist, I know our fearless leader is not above springing a surprise on us just to see how we would react. There's no reason any outsider would put a puzzle into our box."

"Or an insider," Jennifer said. "It's enough of a drag to construct three puzzles a week. My chairman is making nasty remarks about how many papers I haven't published. All this talk about the extra puzzle is garbage."

"I'm sure you're right, Jenny," Karen said, "but you never know. We all have too much invested in the Project to let *anything* disrupt it now."

"You're making mountains out of molehills, K.K.," Bruce said. "I'll never understand why old Humboldt picked you for board monitor."

"What would you do differently, Dr. Yablonski?" Karen asked. "And how do you know what's important? Just stick to your psychological profiles and don't teach me my business."

"Tell me, Dr. Karas," Bruce said. "Why are you so scared of Humboldt?"

"I'm protecting the Project," Karen replied, "and all of you as well. You know how he is when anything doesn't go exactly as planned."

"Maybe Giles Sullivan sent it," Carl said, "as an introduction. Or a test, maybe?"

"If he did," Bruce asked, "why not sign it? He'll be here for the lecture on Sunday; he could just as well have brought it with him."

"If Mr. Sullivan sent it," Dag asked, "why to us? We did not invite him; the Crossword Club did. And how did he know about the Project? And who put the puzzle into the Project's box?"

"Dean Macintosh, probably," Evelyn said. "Giles Sullivan is her boyfriend."

4

"Sourpuss Macintosh?" Jennifer looked skeptical.

"If you didn't give her such a hard time..." Carl said. "She's always been nice to me."

"You're a man," Jennifer replied. "Women her age are afraid of younger ones. Sexual competition is incited by the system to keep us divided."

Evelyn looked at her in disbelief. "Yeah, I guess that's the reason. We really should thank Dean Macintosh for getting us Giles Sullivan. He's a big wheel in the New York Cruciverbal Club. And he's Hannibal's attorney."

"I'd rather have Hannibal himself," Karen said. "His puzzles are super-hard, but they're so clever."

"You can't get Hannibal," Bruce said. "No one's ever seen him, and he never appears in public. But maybe Mr. Sullivan can tell us about him. Could this puzzle have been constructed by Hannibal? For a demonstration?"

"Not a chance," Carl said. "How would he know our methods or our format? Professor Humboldt is very careful about leaks."

"Dr. Macintosh can find out anything she wants," Bruce said. "If she asks, Humboldt has to tell her."

"Nobody," Karen said, "makes Professor Humboldt do anything he doesn't want to do."

"Why are we spending so much time on the seventh puzzle?" Evelyn asked. "It's not worth it. We're all on edge, fighting with one another. Meetings every Monday, Wednesday, and Friday for almost three years, plus all the rest of the work...It'd better pay off, K.K.; I'm not getting any younger."

"If you feel that way," Karen said, "imagine how Dag, Bruce, and I feel. Thank God, it's just a few more weeks."

"Would you please pass out the puzzles and let us get to work?" Jennifer said impatiently. "We've wasted enough time already."

Karen began passing out the sets of test puzzles. "What are you going to do about the seventh puzzle?" Bruce asked.

"I'll make a copy for each of you right after this session and put it into your personal pigeonhole—in case it was

ACROSS

1 Begging vagrant
6 Duke's subordinate
13 It sticks
15 Preventive measure?
16 Part of EKG
17 Microscopic aquatic creature
18 Lacerate
19 Sequel designations
20 "Three men ___ tub"
21 Footsoldiers' grp.
22 Clue to Crusoe
25 Filmdom's M. Hulot
27 Drawing straws, e.g.
28 Palimpsest factor
30 Microprocessor, e.g.
32 Charley Weaver's home, Mt. ___
33 Man's name meaning "a gift"
37 Places

38 "___ answer turneth away wrath"
40 Subject or object, often
41 Makes a choice
43 Result of suppuration
44 Goes off
45 Up
47 Actor Alistair
48 Uris's ___ 18
50 Traveling to the hotel?
54 Horn: French
55 Rounded nut
57 End for den or men
58 Cause for "sudden death"
59 Half a phrase for "intermittent"
61 Transition area
63 Brain section
64 Pulled a Delilah on?
65 Scarlett's farewell?
66 Mt. Rushmore face

DOWN

1 Sting's group
2 Part of R&R, for short
3 Mondrian, e.g.
4 Have it coming
5 Tourney arrangements?
6 Pavan or Berenson
7 In due time
8 Takes turns
9 On the ___ vive
10 Incompetent
11 Boadicea's people
12 Feudal slave
13 "What's My Line?" panelist
14 Medley
23 Of local interest
24 Jimmy
26 Spider
29 Watches Baby
30 Key, in Calais

31 Day off: Abbr.
32 Romanian city
34 Co-ed quarters
35 ___ Town
36 Hosp. personnel
39 Inducing the most laughter
42 Gay refrain
46 One if by land, e.g.
47 Stored the fodder
48 Mercenary's purpose
49 Muslim decree
51 Revenge: German
52 Fellini-based Broadway hit
53 Turned right
54 Rooster's pride
56 Urbana banner abbr.?
60 Bloke
62 Lincoln's fourth son

Puzzle No. 1

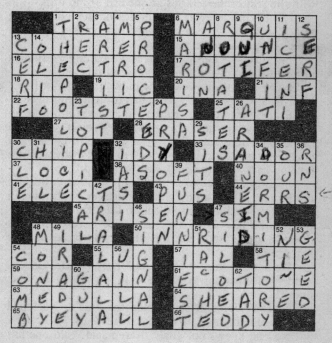

meant for us to solve. Bring the solutions to the Wednesday session, and if we have time, we'll discuss it then. The original goes to Professor Humboldt."

"You'll give it to him directly?" Evelyn looked surprised.

"I'm not going to get my head torn off," Karen said, "for not following procedures. I'll give it to Mrs. Wagner with the rest of the puzzles so she can stamp it in."

"I would like a report from Professor Humboldt," Dag said, "on when we can announce our results. It's been three months since he was here."

"I'm sure he's busy," Karen said, "putting everything in final form. Let's not make waves at this late date."

"I wish he had allowed me to publish a paper or two," Evelyn said. "I've been getting flak from my colleagues."

"Bruce, Dag, and I," Karen said, "are in a worse position. If anything goes wrong with the Project, you three can publish like crazy next year, but we're completely dependent on Professor Humboldt to justify why we were holding back until the book was published."

"Suppose," Bruce said, "my tenure committee decides my Project papers aren't good enough for publication in the professional journals. What do I do then?"

"It's too late now," Dag said. "We have to see this through to the end. But this secrecy is professionally harmful to us."

"We have to keep it all secret," Karen said. "Do you want some other university's team to work along the same lines?"

"Secret?" Jennifer said. "Half the kids in Rockfield have been doing our puzzles for three years."

"No one knows our goal," Karen said. "No one has our results or statistical analyses. And no one knows we're going to submit the Project for the Liberman Prize."

"Big deal," Bruce said. "If we win, it'll be announced a year from now. And my one-twelfth share of the money is eight big hundred dollars."

"It's the prestige that counts," Carl pointed out.

"Meanwhile," Bruce replied, "Humboldt's keeping

everything in his own hands. The papers I wrote are worthless without the other work to back them up."

"Professor Humboldt is as meticulous about the Project as he is about everything else," Karen said. "And as long as he's on our tenure committees, I'm not worried. He has more influence than any other three chairmen put together."

"I just hope he stays healthy," Carl said. "For another few weeks at least."

 **2**

"**P**ACKING ALREADY, OLIVER?" GILES SULLIVAN asked. "But it's only Tuesday."

"I will be spending much of the week preparing for our journey, sir. We must be at the airport at precisely noon Saturday."

"It's only for two nights, Oliver."

"May I point out, sir, that a gentleman who has never packed for himself is hardly qualified to judge. He jests at scars who never felt a wound, sir."

"The melodrama is uncalled for, Oliver. Vermont is hardly the Western Front or the Mato Grosso."

"I *know* what to expect in the Mato Grosso, sir. But if Windham University is anything like Oxford or Cambridge, one may expect the unexpected."

"I am sure," Giles pressed on, "that even I could pack two small bags in an hour."

"I was planning on the four large cases, sir."

"Those huge ones, Oliver? Four of them? We're not going to be presented to the Queen, you know."

"I have noted a tendency in the provinces to overdress, sir, under the misapprehension that is what visitors from the city are accustomed to."

"All right, Oliver, one for informal clothes and one for fancy dress; two suitcases for me. One for you. That leaves one unexplained."

"Equipment, sir. Communications gear. Devices. Various appointments and contrivances. And a few small weapons."

"The whole armory, Oliver? For Vermont?"

"Only the lightest-weight paraphernalia, sir. The minimum quantity at that."

"Sounds like enough to fight an army."

"A *small* army, sir. Preferably ill-equipped."

"You no longer trust your unarmed-combat skills?"

"Unarmed combat requires proximate contact, sir; it is not very effective beyond arm's length. You must have noted too, sir, that I am no longer young. It is difficult for me to run away."

"That has always been difficult for you, Oliver, for which much thanks. But what about your personal equipment, Oliver? The cosh, the knives, the garrote, the boots...? The God knows what else? Don't you *always* carry those?"

"Of limited and specialized use, sir; who can tell what perils await us in Vermont?"

Giles sighed. "Very well, then, Oliver, I give up. What is the point you are trying to make?"

"Your special gold-headed cane, sir. It is inappropriate for you to carry it."

Giles stiffened. "I would feel helpless without it, Oliver. It saved my life in the Brundage murder case."

"Far be it for me to differ with you, sir, but from my viewpoint it not only caused you a great deal of difficulty from which your brother, Percival, had to extricate you; it prevented me from apprehending the killer without bloodshed."

"You wish to make me completely dependent on you, Oliver? Is that it?"

"That would be ideal, sir. A weapon in the hand of an untrained non-killer is extremely dangerous. There is a tendency to assume that one is immune to injury, combined with an unconscious desire to use the weapon. This leads to a neglect of the use of intelligence, which is your real function in our little group."

"I may have to protect Isabel one day."

"If it is insufficiently satisfying, sir, that you are the mysterious Hannibal, nemesis of crossword solvers, consider your position as premier cryptanalyst for our secret little group, selected by Barca himself."

"This is all very well, Oliver, but hardly pertinent."

"Would you really have preferred the days of yore, sir? With yourself as a paladin and Miss Macintosh in the clutches of an evil dragon? Really, sir! Was not your role as a leading criminal attorney sufficient unto the day?"

"I am not a child, Oliver."

"Romance dies hard, sir, and age is no impediment to fantasy. Do you doubt that I would protect Miss Macintosh more efficiently than you? I am now empowered to do so, you know."

"You won't always be there, Oliver. I will."

"I can sleep on the living room couch, sir."

"There is no living room, Oliver. The cabin is a single large room with a bathroom in one corner. Miss Macintosh designed and built it herself."

"If required, I could sleep in the bathtub, sir."

"Isabel felt it would be inappropriate. And I have decided to keep my cane. Shall we drop the childish pouting, Oliver?"

"Yes, sir. Would you be kind enough to help me carry the special bag up to the ground floor on Saturday, sir? It is far too heavy for me."

 **3**

"**B**UT I'M ONLY THREE MINUTES EARLY," KAREN KARAS pleaded with Humboldt's secretary. "Can't you let me in now?"

"The professor said"—Virginia Wagner pursed her cupid's-bow lips—"that he wanted to see you at nine. It is not yet nine."

"I have a class at nine-thirty and it's at the other end of the campus. Does he have anyone else in there now?"

"That is none of your concern, Dr. Karas." To Virginia Wagner, Karen thought, there was only one professor in the whole university. "I will announce you at nine."

"It's Professor Karas to you, Wagner"—Karen leaned her tall body on the secretary's desk—"and you'd better show some respect. I'm not here because I want to be. Professor Humboldt won't like it if you keep me out here."

"The professor needs me more than he needs you," Mrs. Wagner said smugly, patting a loose strand into her metallic-gold bouffant, "so don't go threatening me." She studied her watch and, as the minute hand hit the twelve, said, "You may go in now."

13

Professor Fabian Humboldt had a big voice for such a small man. "Don't sit down, Professor Karas; this will just take a moment."

Although Karen had been there many times, she still marveled at the incongruities of the office. The four walls were covered with photos and drawings of implements of destruction, ancient and modern, ballistae and battleships, Bren guns and bombers. The weapons made a sharp contrast to the neatly dressed professor staring nearsightedly through his thick glasses.

"Yesterday," he said, "you brought me an extraneous crossword puzzle along with the regular Monday assignment of Project work. Who submitted that puzzle?"

"I don't know, Professor; it was in the pigeonhole with the other puzzles."

"When Dr. Richter picked them up, did he notice anything unusual? Some outsider putting something into the box?"

"I didn't ask directly, but he would have mentioned it if he had."

"Professor Karas"—Humboldt was at his charming best—"Karen, it is very important to me and to the Project that you find out who put that puzzle into the box. Or rather"—a thought seemed to strike him—"who constructed that puzzle."

"We discussed it yesterday; some thought you might have done it. To test us."

"Have you ever known me to deviate from established procedure? Obviously it was someone connected with the Project. Who else would know enough to—? Tell the others that if the person who constucted the seventh crossword will make himself"—he stared at Karen for a moment—"or herself known to me and will withdraw the—the puzzle, I will take no heed of the incident. However"—his voice got even louder—"however, if he does not, I will ferret out his identity and the consequences will be dire. Dire!"

Karen couldn't help a slight shiver. "Do you want the—that person to come to your house?"

"I discharge all my social obligations at my annual gathering. Other than that, I will brook no visitors, especially on matters of business. You should know that by now."

"Then how can he communicate with you directly, Professor? You don't talk on the phone, and Mrs. Wagner reads all your correspondence and screens all your visitors. If he sent you the puzzle instead of handing it to you directly, maybe he didn't want to face you for some reason."

"That is logical, Professor Karas. I will instruct Mrs. Wagner to deliver to me, unopened, any sealed envelope with the name of one of you six signed across the flap."

"I'll tell them all. But they—we all have been concerned because you haven't spoken with us directly for weeks. How is the Project going?"

"I am satisfied; everything is on schedule. I have been extremely busy the past several months preparing. Tell them not to worry; the Project will achieve everything I had hoped for, soon. Unless, that is"—he stopped smiling—"you do not remove from me the problem of the seventh puzzle. If I have to devote my time to its solution, I may not be able to carry on my work for the Project. Do I make myself clear, Professor?"

"Yes, sir, very clear. One more thing, my own problem. And Dag Norstad's and Bruce Yablonski's. Tenure. Are you sure—we have so much riding on this, our whole lives—are you sure that we, all three of us, will be granted tenure?"

"I was sure, Assistant Professor Karas, before the seventh crossword arrived. Now I would say it all depends on your finding who constructed that puzzle."

"But that's—"

"Unfair? Then I shall put it another way. It takes a great deal of time and energy, and a great deal of persuasion, to influence the other members of the three tenure committees to grant tenure to applicants with such poor records of publication as you and your colleagues have. If I have to devote my time and energy to finding the constructor of that puzzle myself, I doubt that I will be able to devote sufficient time to...Do I make myself clear? You may leave now, Dr. Karas."

Close to tears, Karen turned to go, then, at the door, turned back. "Does anyone but the eight of us know about the Project?"

"Eight? Oh, you mean me and Mrs. Wagner? No. Definitely not."

"Should I consider Mrs. Wagner a suspect too?"

"Mrs. Wagner?" He thought for a moment. "I don't believe she has the capacity to...Yes, you may consider her too. Definitely. But don't tell her I said so."

4

"**B**OY, ARE YOU IN TROUBLE," AGATHA PARROT SAID
as Isabel Macintosh flopped limply into the office chair.

"Just the good news this early, Aggie. Especially today." Isabel's groan was muffled. "I may have terminal
hangover."

Agatha looked down her hawk nose at her pale-green
boss. "I thought your weakness was egg creams and hot
chocolate."

"Mavis Jordan doesn't know what an egg cream is,"
Isabel said, "and if she did, she wouldn't allow one into
the house. Brandy Alexanders are as close as she gets."

"You got what you deserved, Izzy. Five brandy Alexanders and a fifth of champagne? What else did you expect? So don't complain when the wages of sin come
home to roost."

"Your spies know the color of my garter belt too, Aggie?"

"Black, with red rosettes on the straps," Agatha said
complacently. "Though who you were wearing it for is

17

beyond me. Nothing but professors and administrators at Fathead's Monday nights."

"I wore it for my own soul, Aggie; it's been *months* since I felt like a femme fatale. Can't you confine your spying to my professional life?"

"It's for your own good, Missy. If it wasn't for my intelligence apparatus, you couldn't handle one-tenth the problems around here. Just remember who picked you up out of the gutter and elevated you to dean of faculty."

"Full professor of English literature is not quite the gutter."

"That wasn't what you said five years ago, Miss Ungrateful."

"All right, I owe it all to my faithful Gray Eminence. I will never forget how much I owe you, especially with you reminding me three times a day before meals."

"Don't get snippy with me, young lady. You could easily find yourself teaching remedial reading to assistant professors."

"I'm really grateful, Aggie," Isabel apologized. "You know I can't do without you."

"Sure I know, but I like to hear it out loud once in a while. Even a dog likes a pat on the head now and then."

"Pat, pat." Isabel squinted at her secretary. "I can now focus one eye. What's on the agenda for today?"

"To begin with, you can figure out how to get back into Mavis Jordan's good graces again. Her Hubby may be Fathead to everyone on the faculty but to the board of trustees, Morehead Olcott Jordan is still president of Windham University."

"I never gave a damn before what that pompous poltroon thought; why should I care now?"

"Fathead is retiring next year."

"I've heard *that* before."

"The announcement will be made next week. I have it on the lowest authority."

"You reading entrails, Aggie? Or is it your grandfather's spirit again?"

"Don't laugh, Miss Smartypants. My great-grandfather

was the most respected medicine man in the Five Nations. He wasn't above lifting a paleface scalp either if somebody gave him any lip."

"All right, all right, I'm a believer; he's been right too many times before. But why should this concern me?"

"You're going to be the next president of Windham University. I have spoken."

"I am? Me?" Isabel sat up slowly, holding her head firmly in place with both hands. "I don't want to be president of anything. I've been thinking of going back to teaching."

"You don't have any choice, Miss Macintosh. Not only have I decided, but I've already discussed it with the secretaries of three of the trustees. If you fink out, the job's going to go to Carter Whitbread Somerhill the Third."

"That moron?"

"He's been sucking up to Fathead Jordan ever since he took your place as dean of students."

"Over my dead body will The Third ever—"

"Right. So just start being nice for a change. To *everybody*. Especially Mavis Jordan; he still talks to her, you know. Or, at least, listens."

"What did I do to her last night? I don't remember very much after the champagne."

"You know how she's always calling Fathead 'Hubby'? My 'Hubby' this and my 'Hubby' that?"

"Yeah, it's sickening to see a woman her age acting cutesy-poo."

"With her it ain't acting; she's a genuine world-class cutesy-poo. So what do you think you said when Mavis coyly asked who is the male visitor who is going to be staying at your cabin this weekend?"

Isabel thought for a moment, then turned even paler. "I didn't, Aggie. Tell me I didn't."

"Loud and clear enough to be heard in Bennington. 'He's my *Hobby*,' said Miss Isabel Macintosh, ex-respected dean of faculty."

"She didn't quietly pass over this slight faux pas?"

"Not our Mavis, she didn't. After a short lecture on

19

brazen, drunken hussies came a medium-length editorial on the professional requirements for persons in authority, finishing off with a sermon on who is going to set an example for our innocent young students."

"Innocent? Ha! She should spend an hour in the dean of students' office. Or my office."

"It isn't what goes on, Izzy; it's what's *perceived* as going on."

"Okay, Aggie, how do I get out of this one?"

"When your Hobby, Giles Sullivan, comes this Saturday—he is handsome, mature, and distinguished-looking, isn't he?"

"Very. Except he doesn't look any older than I do. Slim, tall, iron-gray hair—like Cary Grant. You've never seen him?"

"How could I? Every time he's visited you before, you whisked him off to your cabin and neither of you saw the light of day until he left. Afraid I'll steal him from you?"

"I wouldn't put it past the Wicked Witch of the North, but the reason should be obvious. I can be with him only a few times a year, and I don't want to waste a moment on non-essential activities."

"This time you'd better. I'll make the arrangements with Fathead's secretary. The clans will convene on Saturday night at the president's mansion to honor our distinguished guest, Mr. Giles Sullivan, Esquire, renowned criminal attorney and famous solver of crimes."

"One crime, Aggie, the Brundage murder."

"Which stumped the stupid police until Sherlock Sullivan . . . Let me do this my way, Izzy. Mr. Sullivan will be very attentive and gallant—he does know how to kiss hands, doesn't he?" Isabel nodded. "He will be so charmed by our lovely Mavis that he will offer to give a private lesson to her right then and there, but with a sly glance at Fathead he will also invite a few of Mavis's cronies—for appearance's sake, you understand—for a private lesson in crossword solving. Then again, Mavis will never put on her glasses if a man is around. What else can Sullivan do?"

"Forget about *that*, Aggie; I need every bit of strength

he can muster. He was a champion fencer once. Will that do?"

"Only if he stabs Fathead Jordan. Does he dance?"

"Old-fashioned only—waltz and tango. He's good too."

"Perfect. I'll pass the word around that he taught Valentino. Mavis won't be able to keep her hot little hands off him."

"He's not that old, Aggie," Isabel protested. She thought for a moment, then gave in. "All right. I'll sacrifice one evening for the cause. What'll I do while he's leching at Mrs. Jordan?"

"You entertain Mr. Jordan."

"Meaning my black garter belt with the rosettes?"

"He's seen that already, Missy; you were *lots* of fun last night. This time it's a simple black gown and a short string of pearls. Low heels. You don't want to be taller than most of the men there. And stick to white wine. Sip it. Slowly."

"The things I do for Dear Old Windham." Isabel sighed. "Okay, I'll be nice to Fathead. What else do you and your gang of four have in store for me?"

"That's on a need-to-know basis, Izzy. You'll find out when the time comes." Agatha turned serious. "Why is Mr. Sullivan bringing his butler with him this time? And why does the butler have to stay so close to your cabin?"

Isabel hesitated. "It's—conditions have changed. Giles has to take Oliver with him wherever he goes now, even when he visits me. In fact, Oliver wanted to stay in my cabin, which would have dampened the spontaneity somewhat. Did you find him a room near my place?"

"Closest room available was the spare bedroom in my house. The one next to my bedroom."

"Aggie, you're shameless."

"Sure am. It's been a long time since I had a man in my house. He's not too young, is he?"

"No, he's just the right age for you, but I'm not sure. . . . As far as I know, which is not very much, he's led a celibate life for the past fifteen years."

"Leave that to me, Izzy. There was a time I could have had any man in Rockfield, and damn near did. Thanks be to God and jogging, I still have my figure. In an emergency I can always dig out Grandpa's medicine bag; hasn't failed me yet."

"Eye of newt and toe of frog?"

"That's old-fashioned. Grandpa's recipes are strictly vegetarian. Natural herbs and spices, no artificial ingredients."

"You have my best wishes, Aggie. Anything you can do to keep Oliver away from Giles and me this weekend would be greatly appreciated."

"If Oliver is halfway worthwhile, you won't even know he's around."

"I'll do the same for you someday, Aggie." She opened the other eye. "Might as well get to work. What's on for this morning?"

"To begin with, Virginia Wagner called me at home this morning. The eminent Professor Humboldt will be here— she didn't ask, mind you; she just *told* me—here in"— Agatha checked her watch—"in six minutes to inform you of the disgustingly lax security arrangements on campus which permit anyone, repeat, anyone, to put unsought and improper communications into a pigeonhole that is the personal property of the university's most eminent professor."

"Tell him to see Frank Quesada; I'm not head of security."

"You tell him," Agatha said.

"That bad, huh? I thought you weren't afraid of anyone."

"I'm not, but with him I might forget I'm a lady and only one-sixteenth Indian. I'm too old to go to jail."

"Okay, I'll draw his sting. Next?"

"Two girls, one after the other."

"Girls? Students?"

"One undergrad, one graduate school."

"Tell them to see the dean of students. Or if they want a woman, the assistant dean. Pregnant?"

"Pregnant. But they want you, Isabel."

"Come on, Aggie, I don't have time to— By professors?"

22

"You're awfully slow today, Izzy. Why else would I make the appointments. And one after the other?"

"The same professor? Two at once?" Isabel put her head back into her hands.

"Next, your favorite and mine, Assistant Professor of Third World Studies, Jennifer Zapata."

"What the hell does she want this time?" Isabel snarled.

"Not want, Izzy, demand. Guaranteed tenure next year, in effect. Community service, which is what she calls what she does, to be accepted in lieu of publication."

"She's crazy. That would overturn all the accepted standards for awarding tenure, for scholarship. They'd pull our accreditation."

"She'll have lots of support in some circles."

"This is one time I'm going to enjoy meeting with her. I want you on an open intercom with a tape recorder."

"It'll be a pleasure. Then there's lunch with Carter Whitbread Somerhill the Third at the faculty lounge."

"Are you trying to make me lose weight, Aggie? I put up with a lot from you, but—"

"Trust me. He's going to try—you won't believe this—he's going to try to enlist your support for his candidacy as our next Fuehrer. Kid him along and find out what he knows. Order expensive and make him pick up the tab. Flatter him too. He still doesn't know he's a jerk."

"That's some morning you've set up for me, Aggie. What delights are in store for me this afternoon?"

"Just a few committee meetings: salaries, summer session, and affirmative action. Also Fathead wants to set up a committee on drugs and drinking."

"That's not my table. Did you tell him to give it to The Third?"

"It's yours, all right. Some of our younger assistant professors are now—"

There were three firm evenly spaced knocks on the door to Aggie's office. "That has to be Fabian Humboldt the Great," Agatha said. "Get into your office quick. I'll hold him, tell him how wonderful he is for long enough for you to run a comb through your hair and touch up the lipstick. You'll want to make a presentable corpse."

❊❊❊❊❊❊❊❊❊❊❊❊❊❊❊❊❊❊❊❊❊❊ 5 ❊❊❊❊

"I TOLD YOU," KAREN CRIED, "AND NONE OF YOU TOOK it seriously. Bruce even said I was making a mountain out of a molehill."

"I've never seen you lose your cool before," Carl Richter said. "What's going on, K.K.?"

"I had a session with Humboldt this morning that—" She took a deep breath. "I don't know how I got through my classes today. He wants—he *insists* on knowing who put that seventh crossword in the Project box on Monday. And," she added firmly, "so do I."

"What's the big deal?" Jennifer asked. "We've had a thousand puzzles in the Project. One puzzle more or less ... It's all part of this sick, materialistic culture."

"How would you like it"—Karen turned on Jennifer—"if Humboldt killed the whole Project this weekend?"

There were shocked sounds from the whole group. "He can't do that," Evelyn said. "I've neglected everything for the Project. If he kills the Project, I'll never get tenure."

"He cannot just stop the whole Project dead," Dag Norstad said calmly. "We are the Project just as much as he. Do you not all keep copies of the material you turn over to him? I do."

"Of course we do," Bruce Yablonski said. "But he is at the center of everything. Only he has all the data and information. He is integrating it, interpreting it, editing it, making it into a unified book."

"We're specialists," Carl said, "each with the viewpoint derived from our own discipline. None of us is qualified to lead the group, not even K.K. Humboldt is as close to a generalist as you can be these days."

"He also has the title and the fame," Bruce said. "We're unknowns. His name could open doors we don't even know exist."

"And he was making the arrangements with the publisher," Karen pointed out.

"Do you really think," Evelyn asked, "that Professor Humboldt would destroy three years of work just for a stupid little thing like this?"

"You know how rigid he is," Karen said. "The slightest little change in his plans drives him crazy."

"There has to be more to it than that," Bruce said. "As I read his personality, he is not only the most inflexible person I have ever met; he is also a classical anal-retentive, right out of the textbooks. He is grasping, miserly, withholding, especially with money, even though he's far from poor. Remember how he insisted on getting half the money the book brings in?"

"And the six of us split the other half," Jennifer said. "Typical exploitation of labor."

"Bitching again, Jenny?" Carl said. "None of us is in this for the money, at least in the short run. What a scholarly book brings in—my share wouldn't even pay for the paper I used up."

"But that means," Dag commented, "that Professor Humboldt has no financial incentive to keep the Project going. Therefore it behooves us all to do whatever he requires."

"I don't see Humboldt giving up the Project that easily," Bruce said. "It was his own little brainchild and he'd fight to the death not to lose it."

"Dag is right," Karen agreed. "If all he wants is to know who put in the seventh crossword, let's tell him."

"I didn't do it," Bruce said. "But if I had, however innocent my motive, I wouldn't tell."

"Why not?" Evelyn asked. "What's the harm?"

"The harm is that Humboldt is making a big thing out of it. He's so compulsive that if he worked himself up into a big enough rage, he could kill me with one of his fancy weapons just because I made a minor joke."

"It isn't a joke to him," Karen said. "You should have seen his eyes. He even suspects that Virginia Wagner might be involved."

"Voluptuous Virgie, the blond Cerberus?" Bruce laughed. "Can't be. I'm sure she and *Der Fuehrer* have a thing going."

"There's no evidence to that effect," Dag said primly.

"You're evading the issue, Bruce." Karen spoke firmly. "It may be that one of us submitted that puzzle. If so, whoever did it can just admit it, explain that it was an attempt to give Professor Humboldt an interesting puzzle as a gift, anonymously, in appreciation of his efforts on behalf of the Project, and that will be the end of it. Then we can get on with today's session."

There was dead silence. Bruce was carefully studying his colleagues' faces. Jennifer had a smirk on her foxlike little face. Carl sprawled in his chair like a weary bear. Evelyn seemed lost in dreams of her own. Dag stared straight ahead, his face motionless. Karen had an expectant look. Finally Bruce spoke up. "This isn't getting us anywhere. Why don't we examine the puzzle; there must be some clues to the identity of the constructor there. After three years I can usually pick out which one of you made which puzzle."

"Did we all solve it?" Karen asked. There were nods all around. "I thought you were too busy, Evelyn."

"He was very dull, so I cut it short," she said. "Besides,

I couldn't help it. I've been a member of the Crossword Club for years because I love crosswords; I mean, why else? That's one of the reasons Professor Humboldt picked us all for the Project. This one had a few interesting clues; the Project puzzles are boring."

"Only to us, Evelyn," Bruce said. "The little kids love them."

"There were some real weird words," Jennifer said. "Look at 56 Down, 'UILL.' That isn't even in the Oxford Unabridged. The closest I came to it is 'QUILL,' but there's no way the clue fits that."

Evelyn smiled smugly. "That's something you don't learn in Third World Studies, but any academic should know that the University of Illinois is in Urbana. I even thought of a better clue for that: 'uncued pen.'"

"The puzzle's clue is funnier," Karen said quickly, to avoid bloodshed. "If you say it fast, 'Urbana banner abbr.', it sounds like monkeys talking about bananas."

"I completed the puzzle easily," Dag said, "because of the crossings, but I did not understand the clue to 15 Across."

"It's an old American saying," Carl told him. "That's why you didn't get it. 'An ounce of prevention is worth a pound of cure.'"

"65 Across and 64 Across are good clues," Bruce said, "and 5 Down isn't bad, but 50 Across, 'Traveling to the hotel?' That's pretty clumsy. I've seen better in *The New York Times*."

"Exactly," Bruce gloated. "I have it. This puzzle does not *contain* the message; it *is* the message. It tells, if it was done by one of us, that the constructor is capable of interfering with the Project, of throwing a monkey wrench into the machinery. And if it was done by an outsider, it also says that he knows all about the Project."

"If you're right," Evelyn said, "I hope it was an outsider. No wonder Professor Humboldt was upset."

"I'm right, all right," Bruce said smugly. "It all fits. Now, the problem is, I'm sure it was an insider. Why should any of us want to interfere with the Project? We

ACROSS

1 ___ browns
5 Barbershop logo
9 Egg, in combinations
12 "*Vissi d'* ___" from *Tosca*
13 Without joking
14 Author Silverstein
15 Scoff
16 Pinky and thumb?
18 Scouting outing
20 *West Side Story* song
21 Worshipper's place, maybe
22 Folks on the lookout
24 Israeli politico Ariel
27 Gettysburg general
28 Yesterday: Italian
29 Shostakovich or Tiomkin
31 Southern st.
34 Catholic *BROAD*
36 Crossword bird
37 Hardly delicious
39 Porcine parent
40 Culinary garb
43 Baserunner's goal
44 Seafarer's rate
45 They waited for Godot
47 Edits the videotape
50 Spotted
51 Not merely miffed
52 Blanch mink?
56 Headline re a successful bloodhound?
59 Queue
60 Beer containers
61 Big name in labor
62 Make ___ meet
63 Cockney residence
64 Wagner's *Switch* role
65 Laugh-a-minute guy

DOWN

1 Muslims' pilgrimage
2 Space
3 Skiing slowdown maneuver
4 Botany references
5 *Zorro* star
6 Duck in *Peter and the Wolf*
7 "The Lip"
8 One of the Westmores
9 Notoriously busy airport
10 To come: French
11 As ___ the hills
13 Artery of London
14 Arab chief's ice cream treat?
17 With 35 Down, what a choreographer is?
19 *The Story* ___
22 Become embedded
23 Gynotikolobomassophile's target
24 Sometime rivals, for short
25 Submarine
26 One after another *MINOS*
27 Cretan king
30 Emporia
31 Gift-tag word
32 Chester B. Goode's affliction
33 Summertime quenchers
35 See 17 Down?
38 Philip Marlowe's creator . . .
41 . . . and Auguste Dupin's
42 Only beau
44 St. ___-Nevis
46 Member of the fam. .
47 Deranged one
48 Preliminary contest

28

49 Ted of *The Love Boat*
50 Script section
52 Card game for three
53 Done, in Dijon

54 Wreck
55 Whatever's left
57 Elec. unit
58 Average grade

Puzzle No. 2

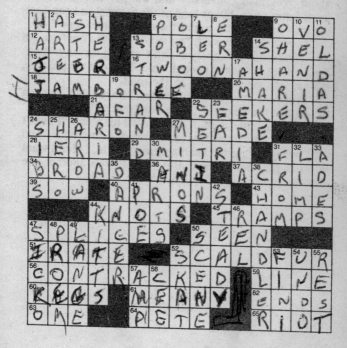

29

all lose if anything goes wrong, lose big."

"Nobody, none of us, really *likes* Professor Humboldt," Carl said.

"Nobody really likes our dear president, Morehead Jordan, either," Bruce said. "And there are lots of things about Windham University and the psychology department I don't like, but as long as the paychecks keep coming in, I'm not about to put them out of business."

"Look," Jennifer said, "nobody's going to confess. All this academic-type analysis isn't getting us anywhere. We've already wasted enough time. Pass out the puzzles, Karas; let's get this show on the road."

"I suppose you're right, Jennifer," Karen said, starting to sort out the puzzles. "Take your places."

"Wait a minute, K.K.!" Carl raised his hand. "I didn't realize at the time this was such a major catastrophe. And then, when we started analyzing the puzzle, I didn't want to break the train of logic. But—but there's another one of those puzzles in today's batch."

 **6**

"**S**TOP FIDGETING," FABIAN HUMBOLDT COLDLY TOLD the six assistant professors gathered in his office. "Mrs. Wagner"—he nodded at his secretary—"will take notes." Karen couldn't help but admire the smooth way he brought the buxom secretary into the group without accusing her of anything.

The six adjusted their positions uncomfortably. Whether it was Humboldt's stiff military bearing that did it, his hard gray eyes, or his staccato speech, Karen wasn't sure, but no one was ever fully at ease with this thin, dry little man. "Mrs. Karas," Humboldt said, "whom I chose as deputy, did not transmit my message strongly enough; that is evident."

"I didn't get the message," Carl Richter explained, "until after I picked up the puzzles from the pigeonhole."

Humboldt glared at Karen. "You had two hours to communicate with only five people after our meeting. Evidently you did not think it important enough to give any of them my message until the time of the meeting. Why?"

"I had no idea, Professor, that there would be a second puzzle—"

"You didn't *think*," Humboldt said flatly. "Incompetent intelligence has been the cause of more lost battles than all the other failures combined. If I were not so short of time..."

"Could it not have been a compliment to you, Professor?" Dag Norstad asked. "A gift of an interesting puzzle, is it not so? Everyone knows how much you like—"

"I do not know how things are done in Norway, Dr. Norstad," Humboldt broke in, "but in civilized society, gifts and compliments are presented face to face, man to man. It is only this sort of contemptible insolence that must be sneaked in anonymously."

"It's only a crossword puzzle, Professor," Jennifer Zapata said. "What's the big deal?"

"I don't often agree with Jenny," Karen said, "but really, Professor, aren't you going to an awful lot of trouble about a couple of simple little crossword puzzles?"

"I once had hope for you, Karen, but since you married your poet, you have sunk back into mediocrity. Can you really not see what these two puzzles represent?"

"I can see that they represent an irritation to you, sir," Bruce Yablonski said. "But I don't see that they're doing any harm."

"A practitioner of your art, Yablonski—none dare call it a science in my presence—is not forbidden to use simple logic." Humboldt's eyes pinned the plump psychologist to the wall. "What do you deduce from these two interlopers and the way they were thrust into the Project?"

"Well"—Bruce was already sweating—Humboldt's merciless interrogations were a campus legend. "They were constructed by someone who had some knowledge of the Project."

"A brilliant exposition, Yablonski. And is it not probable"—Humboldt's voice became theatrically sarcastic—"that this someone had *some* knowledge of English and had *some* access to paper and a typewriter?"

"Yes, sir, of course. I—we—believe it was someone who had access to *inside* knowledge of the Project."

"Yablonski, you wear the clothes of an American male and you grow hair on your chin. A census taker would classify you as a man. I would call you the predictably pitiful result of the effects of permissive parents and progressive education on what was originally a great genetic heritage. The ancient Israelites were a tough, decisive people; they would not easily recognize some of their descendants." Humboldt turned to Karen and snapped, "Karas, who constructed these puzzles?"

"Someone in this room, Professor." She unconsciously stood at attention, eyes straight ahead. "The format exactly matched the puzzles we are producing."

"Who were the puzzles intended for?"

"You, sir. There was no name on either puzzle, so they were not for any of us. Had they been designed for all of us to solve, there would have been six copies of each puzzle."

"Why were the puzzles put into the Project's box?"

"You have no phone at home and never speak on the phone to anyone."

"That is inaccurate, Karas."

"Correction, sir. You respond on the phone only to a small number of people and then only after your secretary gives you the name of the caller and his purpose."

"Incomplete, Karas."

"Yes, sir. Other than *originating* a call from this office, which is placed by your secretary, you will accept calls from only a small number of selected important people who, even then, must give their name and their reason for calling to Mrs. Wagner. You also record all telephone conversations."

"That last was premature, Karas, but pertinent. I will accept it. Now, why were those puzzles not mailed?"

"Mail is slow and uncertain. On your orders, no mail is delivered to your home. Mrs. Wagner opens and sorts all mail and any memos put into your office mail slot. Every piece of paper that comes in is time-stamped."

"Barely adequate, Karas. Not only did you require prompting, but you failed to note that the mysterious caller's voice, had he phoned, might be known to Mrs. Wagner." Humboldt addressed Carl. "Richter, you have been completely silent today. What conclusion can you draw from this?"

"Well, Professor"—the big man shifted from foot to foot—"somebody wants to get a message across to you, and fast, but doesn't want you to know who he is."

"Nothing else, Richter? Did you solve both puzzles?"

"I guess we all did, Professor. There's no message in either one; at least that I can see."

"Then why were they sent, Richter? Idle whim?"

"No sir. Bruce said that the puzzles—the *act* of sending them—that was the message."

Humboldt looked sharply at Bruce. "Yablonski, if the puzzles are the message, what is that message?"

"Assuming that the constructor of the puzzles is one of us," Bruce said hesitantly, "which seems likely," he added quickly at Humboldt's snort of exasperation, "then—"

"Jump, Yablonski," Humboldt barked. "For God's sake, speak up."

"Someone wants to . . . is threatening to . . . to hurt the Project."

"*Destroy*, Yablonski. Not hurt, destroy. Say it."

"Destroy the Project. Yes, sir."

"Any disagreement?" Humboldt looked around the office, peering into each one's eyes for a full second. He did not exclude Virginia Wagner, who colored at his stare. No one said a word. "Like pulling teeth," Humboldt said in a disgusted tone. "And you all want tenure." He put both palms flat on his desk and leaned forward. "Whichever of you sent those puzzles, speak up now. I do not allow myself to be threatened—you should all know that by now—but I will make some concession for a temporary aberration. You will leave the Project at once, of course, but I will allow one year to find a place at another school. Nothing on your record; no recommendation, but no black marks either."

Dead silence. No movement. Only shallow breathing.

"I will arrange anonymity," Humboldt said. "That is as far as I will go." He waited for a moment longer, then said, "Whoever you are, if you wish to destroy the Project, I may very well grant you your wish. I am prepared to lose this time, are you?" He leaned back in his big leather chair. "Very well, then. Carry on with your regular session this afternoon. Mrs. Wagner will inform Karas of my decision Monday morning."

All six let out their breath at once. "You can't—" Karen shouted.

"Can't I?" Humboldt smiled. "Who is to stop me?"

"My tenure," Bruce cried. "All of us. We have our lives invested in the Project."

"Save your life, then," Humboldt said softly. "Expose the villain."

"You're punishing all of us for one guy," Jennifer yelled. "I'll shut down the whole damn campus."

"I'm pleased you subscribe to my methods," Humboldt jeered. "Tell me how that will get you tenure. You haven't published a word since those idiots donated you a doctorate for breathing."

"You promised us a major book." Evelyn seemed on the verge of tears.

"I didn't change the conditions; you did."

Carl Richter stepped forward, eyes red, his huge hands opening and closing spasmodically. "In front of six witnesses, Richter?" Humboldt mocked. "Try using your brain for a change."

The six stood stunned, prisoners who had received the death sentence from a court of no appeal. Humboldt stood up behind his desk. "As I expected. Glandular reactions and no rational thought. You could have learned from me in all these years, but you did not. You could have thought for yourselves, but you did not. You, who claim to be scholars, who aspire to be full professors, who want to be granted tenure—such people should be little lower than the angels, not little higher than the beasts of the jungle. Had you been aware of your inadequacies, had you realized, even, your inability to analyze your situation calmly and rationally, you might have thought to ask my advice."

Karen waved the others to silence. She took a deep,

calming breath. "What do you advise, Professor Humboldt?"

"The obvious," he said quietly. "It is now midday, Friday. You have almost three days. Find the source of your troubles."

"And when we do, Professor? What are we to do? Kill him?"

"Give me the name," Fabian Humboldt said calmly. "I will do the rest."

 **7**

"**I**'VE THOUGHT IT OVER," ISABEL ANNOUNCED LOUDLY as she entered Agatha Parrot's office, "and I'm not going to do it."

"And a very good morning to you, Miss Manners," Agatha said. "What is it you aren't going to do now, besides be civil?"

"I'm not going to be president of Windham," Isabel said. "Good morning. It's nothing but a fund-raising job, practically, and constantly entertaining people I don't like."

"Duty before pleasure," Agatha said. "Where did you learn the facts of life, Sodom and Gomorrah?"

"Not being president of Windham isn't quite the same as endless debauchery. And look who's talking, Mrs. Machiavelli."

"Anything I do is for your own good, Isabel."

"Are you quoting Stalin, Hitler, or Genghis Khan? Now tell me the part where, when I get clobbered, it hurts you more than it hurts me."

"It does, Isabel," Agatha said softly. "It really does.

37

But I love Windham, too, and sometimes... You don't want The Third to become our next president, do you?"

"There must be a hundred other ways to stop him; he's so dumb."

"Stupidity can be a plus in the eyes of some of the trustees. But besides fund-raising, a president has a lot of power too. Do you want to see The Third put into practice his ideas of what a university should be like? And how many times have you wished you could make a few changes of your own?"

"I know, Aggie, but why can't I support an outsider who thinks the way I do? Almost any outsider has a better chance of being selected than an insider. Everybody here already knows everyone else's flaws."

"When there's time for a search, they pick an outsider. Fathead's resignation will be totally unexpected. Even I didn't know it was going to happen."

"Your bootblack-busboy network failed you?"

"It was a sudden decision. Fathead is going to run for the Senate. Mavis decided."

"Are you kidding? Nobody can beat—they're just looking for a sucker candidate."

"Even Mavis knows that, but the exposure, she figures, will lead to an appointment in Washington. Mavis is drooling at the idea of a salon in Georgetown."

"Can't you just see him as Secretary of Education? I think I'd rather have him in the Senate."

"He gets neither," Agatha said, her jaw set. "A harmless minor post with a big title, that's his payoff."

"So," Isabel said, finally sitting down in the big leather chair, "the trustees figure that the next president of Windham will be there only a year or two while they make their real search?"

"They'll be in for a big surprise when you take over."

"It doesn't have to be me; there are lots of people who'd be happy to get paid for not making waves for a year or two. It doesn't have to be a Whitbread Somerhill the Third."

"Oh, they know who to name, all right, if there's too

much opposition to The Third. That's why you have to become president."

"Playing coy again, Aggie? You want me to beg?"

"Just ask politely, Missie. The magic word."

"Please, ma'am, may I know the secret name?"

"I nominate as the next president of Windham University"—Agatha's voice became deep and formal—"a sterling scholar, and a man who has the support of the most powerful organizations in the country, University Professor Fabian Humboldt, Ph.D."

"Oh, God! No! He'd have us doing close-order drill every morning before class. Are you sure, Aggie?"

"Positive. I have it on the lowest authority. Confirmed."

Isabel knew when she was beaten. "All right, puppetmaster," she said with a sigh, "I'll kiss ass. Just tell Mavis Jordan to wash it first. Is the giant soirée set up?"

"Practically. You and Sullivan are invited to the regular Saturday-night VIP bash. Nine P.M. sharp, at the presidential mansion. A dozen rich alumni, at least four trustees, and, to lower the tone a bit, a couple of politicians. Plus their bejeweled wives. And all of Mavis's cronies, so she can lord it over them. Make sure Sullivan brings a black tie."

"He wants to relax; he isn't coming here for a formal wake."

"He is now; the relaxing he can do later. And make sure he mingles with the trustees and charms them with stories about when he was a practicing criminal attorney. They love dirt."

"And me? I'm to be on display at the meat market?"

"Don't make trouble, Izzy. Bring a hip flask of egg creams if you have to, but button your lip. Think whatever you want but positively no feminist foolishness out loud. Say please and thank you and curtsy very sweetly."

"You want Giles to do all my talking for me too?"

"Giles will be busy charming Mavis Jordan. You will not have any beaus, and especially no *hobbies*, hanging around *at all* that night. You will carefully give the old coots who hold the fate of Windham in their bony fingers the firm impression that you usually spend Saturday nights dusting books in the library and checking the petty cash. Is that clear? Small ladylike smiles and sit with your knees together."

Isabel nodded resignedly. "You said *practically*. Does that mean everything is *not* set?"

"Nope. Just that you have one tiny little job to do. Nothing to it."

Isabel eyed her warily. "I always get chills when you go casual on me."

"Really, Isabel." Agatha looked her most innocent. "Nothing at all. It's all your fault anyway. Mavis is still extremely sore at you. She thinks you may have been making fun of her Hubby, which of course you weren't. You were making fun of her, but she could never conceive that. So I had to offer her a very small special inducement."

"My head? On a silver platter?"

"Don't be silly, silly; would I do a thing like that? All I did was tell her that a *real* English butler would serve at her little party."

"Oliver?"

"He is English, isn't he? I mean *really*?"

"Don't change the subject, Agatha Parrot. Oliver isn't coming here to work."

"Of course he is, Izzy, what else? The skiing season is six months off."

"I mean he's not coming up here to work for Mavis Jordan."

"Of course not, sweetie; he's really working for you. And for the dear old blue and gray. Besides, I already promised Mavis he'd be there. Do you want people to think I don't always tell the truth?"

"Agatha, one of these days. . . ."

"Don't hold your breath, dear," Agatha smiled sweetly. "Is it a deal?"

"All right," Isabel said resignedly. "I'll call Giles and ask him to ask Oliver."

"That's nice; kills two birds with one stone."

Isabel was suspicious. "Two birds? What other nasty little trick do you have up your sleeve?"

"I was going to arrange it when they got here, but as long as you're on the phone, you might as well do it."

"Do what?"

"Tell Oliver to put pure vodka in one glass and make sure The Third gets that one."

"That's low, Aggie; brilliant, but low."

"I just want to let him show the trustees his true character," Agatha said innocently. "That's all. Besides, you did practically the same thing last Monday all by your own sweet self. Honestly, Missy, the moment I take my eyes off you..."

"I'd hate to have you for an enemy, Aggie."

"Thank you, dear, I knew you'd see it my way. You can start by not giving me any work this morning."

"I thought you had everything under control."

"I do; oh, I do. Just one more teensy-weensy little problem to solve."

Isabel looked at her blankly. "Which is?"

"How to get rid of Fabian Humboldt, dear."

8

"SOMEONE PUT PLASTIC OVER THE PROJECT'S PIGEONhole," Carl Richter said, "with a note to bring today's puzzles here."

"I did," Karen said. "I want to make absolutely sure I'm not surprised by a *third* seventh puzzle at today's session. I've had enough from Humboldt to last me all year."

"What do I do with my puzzle?" Jennifer asked.

"Come up here and give it to me, and the copies too. I'm going to go through each set to make sure I'm getting only what I'm supposed to get." Karen opened her attaché case and said, "Okay, bring them up to me one at a time." Suddenly she pushed the case to the side of the desk and said, "No, I'll collect them later. Hold on to your assigned puzzles for a while; we have something more important to do first."

"The second puzzle?" Evelyn asked.

"The second *seventh* crossword," Bruce corrected her. "We've only got till Monday to save our lives."

"What did you come up with, Bruce?" Carl asked.

"Nothing. Not a damn thing. You?"

"Well, I noticed how many foreign words were used again," Carl said. "There's '*arte*,' '*ieri*,' '*hajj*,' '*venir*,' and '*fini*.' You could even add '*ovo*,' from the Latin."

"If you will accept proper nouns," Dag said, "there are more foreign words, 'Maria,' 'Sharon,' 'Dmitri,' 'O'Hare,' and 'Kitts.'"

"O'Hare might be considered an American name by now," Karen said. "But you're right; there are an unusually large number of names. Add to what Dag gave, 'Shel,' 'Meade,' 'Meany,' 'Pete,' 'Power,' 'Leo,' 'Ern,' 'Strand,' 'Chandler,' 'Poe,' and 'Lange.' If you stretched things a bit, 'O' is both a name and foreign."

"What do you make of this, Bruce?" Evelyn asked. "The constructor is someone who is impressed by big names? By fame? The kind of guy who reads *People* magazine?"

"There's no doubt about that, Evelyn, but I don't have enough to go on to make a useful personality profile. What I was looking for was feelings, emotion, attitudes. There's very little strong feeling visible here. All I could find with any possible connotation of emotional content was 'sober,' 'jeer,' 'jamboree,' 'seekers,' 'acrid,' 'irate,' 'riot,' 'sibs,' 'hero,' 'steady,' 'rel,' 'sicko,' 'undo,' and 'rest.' A lot of words, although I'm probably stretching things a bit, but very little anger or hatred."

"There is 'irate,' 'riot,' and 'sicko,'" Jennifer said.

"Not enough. And no person we would agree was a sicko would use that word very comfortably."

"Is that not useful information in itself?" Dag asked. "The person who constructed this puzzle was capable of great control of emotion, even though he seems to be threatening the Project."

"And us," Evelyn said. "If it was one of us, he would have to know that Humboldt would take it out on all of us."

"Sometimes when I'm constructing a puzzle," Carl said, "I can't fit in the words I want and have to use some words I don't really want."

"That's the nature of constructing," Karen said. "But

I'm sure that the majority of the words used would be consistent with the character of the constructor."

"He's well educated," Jennifer said. "I didn't know what 'proem' was till yesterday."

"We went through that with the first puzzle," Karen said. "If it's one of us, of course he's educated. We're all Ph.D.'s, we're all assistant professors; three of us are up for tenure this year, three the next."

"That's it," Bruce said. "The first puzzle. We're treating the two puzzles as separate entities. They're not; they're one piece. Let's put the puzzles together, K.K." He pulled his chair up to Karen's desk. "All of us. Do you have a copy of the first puzzle?"

Karen took the sheet from her open attaché case and placed it on the desk. Next to the first puzzle she placed the second. "Some of you will have to read it upside down," she said. "Let's see what we've got."

They pulled their chairs around Karen's desk. "The idea is," Bruce said, "to look at these as one source by combining words from both puzzles into a meaningful message."

A full minute passed, then Evelyn said, "I don't see anything that looks even remotely meaningful."

"I'm beginning to see something," Karen said. "Put this down, Bruce, 'irate,' and 'seekers.' That's from number two. And after that, put '*Rache*'; that's revenge in German. Now '*Mila*,' also from number one, a concentration camp. It's beginning to make sense now." Her voice grew excited. "Here's another pair, 'electro,' and 'amp.'"

"I see one," Carl said. "Put a capital P on 'pole' and after that 'unfit.'"

"Put 'medulla' after 'electro' and 'amp,'" Jennifer added.

"'Sicko,' and 'of O,'" Evelyn said. "*The Story of O* is about torture."

"That's perfect," Karen said. "We've got it."

"Wait," Bruce said. "I have two more, 'anon,' and 'con tracked.'"

"And '*fini*,' from puzzle two, ends it," Dag said.

"There does, indeed, seem to be a very clear message here."

"Let's put it all together now," Karen said. "What do you have written, Bruce?"

"Irate, seekers, *Rache*, *Mila*, electro, amp, Pole, unfit, medulla, sicko, of O, anon, con tracked, *fini*. It will be even better if I rearrange the words and fill in some connectives. Like this. An *anonymous convict* has been *tracked* by *irate seekers* of *Rache* (revenge) for sadistic torture (*of O*) in a concentration camp (*Mila*) by *amps* of *electro*shock applied to the *medulla* of *unfit Poles* by a *sicko* who is now *fini*."

"Wow," Jennifer said. "Now I know why old Humboldt was so sore. He was scared they'd drag him off to Israel, like Eichmann. The puzzle isn't against the Project; it's against Humboldt."

"I always knew he was a Nazi at heart," Bruce said. "I used to call him *Der Fuehrer*, and I guess I subconsciously knew."

"And look at his books and lectures," Jennifer pointed out. "Always about how great war is. Typical."

"Humboldt must have solved this before he called us in this morning," Carl said. "Why did he go through the charade?"

"Making us think the medium was the message?" Evelyn asked. "Maybe he didn't know what the message said."

"Are you kidding, Evelyn?" Carl said. "He's the best puzzler in New England. If we found the message, he sure as hell did. No, what I was talking about was his making us go through the whole rigamarole of finding who the constructor was, when he knew who all the time."

"Well, that's his way," Karen said, "to make someone else do his dirty work for him."

"What are you talking about?" Jennifer asked. "Do you really know who the guy is?"

"Well, of course," Carl said. "It's Bruce. Yablonski's the only Polish name around here."

"Wait a minute," Bruce yelled. "Just wait a minute. I'm not Polish; I'm American. Besides, I'm Jewish."

ACROSS

1 Moon Child's symbol
5 Disconcert
10 Cry from the crow's-nest
14 Daughter of Eurytus
15 Moderately: slang
16 Celebes ox
17 Captured
18 Notions-counter purchase
19 Phaser setting
20 *Star Wars* government
22 Twisting a caraway seed?
24 He was McGarrett
26 Puzzling situation
27 Ruling principles
31 Geisel villain
35 Diamond stat.
36 Gymkhanas
38 Businesswomen's award
39 Peculiar bloke
41 1945 Johnny Mercer song
43 Senior's cause for panic

44 Spot on the map
46 Great Lake tribe
48 Seagoing flyer
49 Which letter is downbeat?
51 Imperfect circles
53 Andy's son
55 Unmatched
56 Kits for carpenters
60 *Sound of Music* song
64 Portoferraio's island
65 Oriental board game
67 Fruity desserts
68 Tend a typo
69 Rib
70 Query re bad handwriting:
   "Are these t's, e's,
   ___?"
71 Apportion
72 Polonius's cache
73 Obligation to make tea,
   you say?

DOWN

1 Give as an example
2 Breathing space
3 Trimmed, so to speak
4 Dress as a Scot?
5 Said for sure
6 Lauper song, "She ___"
7 Lined up
8 Airborne perambulator,
   maybe
9 Forcing to go
10 When to use mascara?
11 Unfavorable voter
12 Proper subject, at times
13 Ozarkese expletive
21 Gad about
23 Went like 60
25 Tractor man John
27 Ledger loss
28 March 17 celebrants
29 Honkytonk pianist
   Frankie

30 Cubic meter
32 Puts the kibosh on
33 County of Erin
34 *Magnificat* and
   Benedictus
37 Harbor sights
40 Lonely
42 Airs
45 Unreported income, often
47 Missile shelter
50 Z's in Xochimilco
52 Spot of ink
54 Choice of solvent?
56 Abound
57 Ye ___ Shoppe
58 Postmortem bio
59 Take to the skies
61 Wallpaper shade
62 Liquefy
63 Suburb of Paris
66 Troop group: Abbr.

Puzzle No. 3

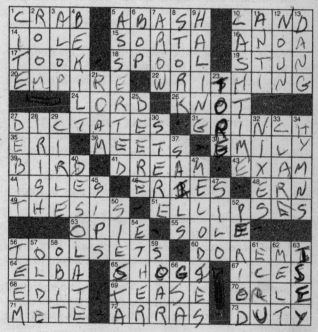

The completed crossword grid reads:

Row 1: C R A B · A B A S H · L A N D
Row 2: I O L E · S O R T A · A N O A
Row 3: T O O K · S P O O L · S T U N
Row 4: E M P I R E · W R I T H I N G
Row 5: · L O R D · K N O T ·
Row 6: D I C T A T E S · G R I N C H Y
Row 7: E R I · M E E T S · E M I L Y
Row 8: B I R D · D R E A M · E X A M
Row 9: I S L E S · F R I E S · E R N
Row 10: T H E S I S · E L L I P S E S
Row 11: · O P I E · S O L E ·
Row 12: T O O L S E T S · D O R E M I
Row 13: E L B A · S H O G I · I C E S
Row 14: E D I T · T E A S E · O R L E
Row 15: M E T E · A R R A S · D U T Y

"That makes the cheese more binding," Carl said. "Your father was Polish, wasn't he? Or of Polish descent? Your mother, too, probably."

"Yeah, and your father was German," Bruce shot back. "He was probably even a Party member."

"Don't tell me you didn't have any relatives in Poland," Carl said, "who were killed in concentration camps."

"Of course I did," Bruce replied, "and so did millions of other Jews and Poles and almost any other nationality in America. That doesn't mean I'm part of a revenge squad."

"No, but you might be helping them," Carl said, "by writing these warnings to Humboldt."

"What about Dag?" Bruce said. "The Nazis occupied Norway too."

"Dag's English isn't good enough," Carl said, "to allow him to construct a crossword with a message in it."

"My English is perfect," Dag said, "but I didn't construct the puzzles. No Norwegian did. You must remember, it said 'Poles.'"

"Let's not fight among ourselves," Karen said. "We don't know if we're right; what we have now is conjecture."

"If you think so"—Carl was still red-faced—"why don't you try to get a different message out of the puzzles?"

"I don't see one right now," Karen said, "but there may be one, completely different, that we haven't found yet."

"Statistically," Dag said, "we have about one hundred fifty words here, so it is likely that there is more than one message to be found merely by taking enough samples at random."

"Monkeys at a typewriter?" Carl jeered.

"Even if the message we extracted," Karen said, "is correct, there may be a completely different interpretation that can be placed on it."

"You're always standing up for that little fascist," Jennifer said. "Why don't you face facts, Karas? The man's a menace. He's got to go. Let's confront him."

"Maybe we will, Jennifer, and if we decide to do it,

I'll be the first in line. But first"—Karen turned toward Bruce—"if you constructed those puzzles, come talk to me later, at my home. Call first, and I'll send my husband to a movie or something. We'll figure out some way so that Professor Humboldt won't stop your tenure. If he really is a disguised Nazi, we can use that information to pressure him."

"Not just Bruce, Karas," Jennifer said. "We all get tenure, okay? We all stick together, right? Take collective action against that bastard."

"Don't hold your breath waiting for my call, K.K." Bruce looked sullen. "I didn't do it, period."

"I'll be home most of the evening anyway," Karen said "just in case you change your mind. Or if you'd rather go directly to Professor Humboldt's house by yourself, well, you know where it is."

"Look. I've got an important meeting at six," Jennifer said. "We spent a lot of time finding the message today; can we leave the regular session for tomorrow, maybe?"

"I'm afraid not," Karen said. "Let's not have any more trouble with Professor Humboldt. Push your chairs back and let's get started. Hand me your puzzles one by one. I'll sort them, and we'll start right away."

There was a small bustle as the five crowded around Karen's desk. Karen checked each set of puzzles and copies as it was handed to her. She pulled over her attaché case and took out her set. She glanced into the case, hesitated, then took out a single sheet. Karen took a deep breath and gasped, "Oh, God! There's another puzzle in my attaché case. What are we going to do now?"

The other five clustered around Karen's desk again. She waved them off and said tiredly, "I'll make copies right away. One goes to Virginia Wagner immediately, and right after that I'll put one into each of your pigeonholes. Please pick up your copy and solve the puzzles tonight. We'll meet here tomorrow at nine sharp. And I mean *sharp*."

◼◼◼◼◼◼◼◼◼◼◼◼◼◼◼◼◼◼◼◼◼◼ 9 ◆◆◆

"**T**HAT WAS AN EXCELLENT DINNER," GILES SAID, PUTting down his napkin. "Ping has outdone himself again."

"He will be gratified to hear it, sir; he wasn't sure you would approve of the ingredients."

Giles looked up apprehensively. "Couldn't you have asked me before I ate?"

"It might have interfered with your full enjoyment of the authentic dishes. Ping spent a good deal of time on research and shopping."

"Then you shouldn't have—" Giles sighed. "Very well then, since we are discussing food, Isabel asked me to ask you to—"

"Yes, sir, I understand. You may tell Miss Macintosh, sir, that I will be pleased to cooperate, although in my experience the results of an overdose of ethyl alcohol are too unpredictable for sound planning. If she were to be more specific as to her requirements, I could administer a judicious mixture of some of my—"

"I don't think Mrs. Jordan would appreciate one of her guests suddenly growing fangs and claws."

"What I had in mind, sir, was a sudden attack of un-inhibited absolute truthfulness, which is guaranteed to make an enemy of anyone within hearing."

"I think not, Oliver; we don't want to call too much attention to you."

"I have available a variety of—"

"Just the vodka, Oliver, if you please."

"As you say, sir. But I will accept no responsibility if Mr. Somerhill's reaction does not fit Miss Macintosh's requirements exactly."

"Must you listen to *every* conversation I have with Miss Macintosh?"

"I am pleased you understand, sir. Though if I may be so bold, sir, perhaps your chats might be a bit less lengthy? I was near the end of a particularly baffling whodunit when Miss Macintosh rang."

"It is always possible to hang up, Oliver, if the conversation is not as fascinating as the latest gory opus. Or even, perish the thought, not to pick up the phone?"

"One's conscience might chafe at the dereliction of duty. What is worse, sir, you might, in the grip of some powerful but misguided emotion, commit us to a course of action which, had your hormones been more passive, you might never have considered."

"Put the thought out of your head, Oliver; I am old enough to know better."

"I quite agree, sir, but Miss Macintosh is an extraordinary woman."

"Miss Macintosh is the most sensible woman I have had the good fortune to meet in fifteen years."

"Miss Macintosh is often quite impulsive too, sir. She is fortunate in having Miss Parrot attending her. I have the impression she is a highly practical person."

"You will have the opportunity of meeting her tomorrow, Oliver. From what Isabel has told me of Miss Parrot, you should find the encounter quite interesting and even exciting."

"I find all of life interesting, sir. But for excitement, I'm afraid I must turn to my whodunits."

✖✖✖✖✖✖✖✖✖✖✖✖✖✖✖✖✖✖✖✖✖✖ 10 ✖✖✖✖

"Iᴛ'ꜱ ᴛʜʀᴇᴇ ᴍɪɴᴜᴛᴇꜱ ᴀꜰᴛᴇʀ ɴɪɴᴇ, Zᴀᴘᴀᴛᴀ," Kᴀʀᴇɴ said sharply. "You knew this was a vital meeting. Can't you ever do things right?"

"You're beginning to sound more and more like old Humboldt," Jennifer replied. "It's Saturday. What's the big deal about three minutes?"

"Let's see what kind of small deal you make, Zapata," Evelyn said, "when you're turned down for tenure next year."

"I don't want any needling from you either, Tinguely," Karen said. "We have serious work to do. Pull your chairs around my desk and let's get right to work. And just in case, I made sure to get here first, and my attaché case is under my chair, locked. I don't want to see anything on the table but your solved puzzle and a scratch pad."

"Do you really think there'll be a fourth puzzle?" Bruce asked.

"I don't think anything," Karen said. "I'm just playing it safe."

"It is extremely improbable," Dag said, "that there will be another puzzle. Whatever effect these puzzles were intended to have has certainly been achieved, I am sure."

"Quit wasting time," Jennifer said. "I have an important meeting at ten. I didn't get anything out of this puzzle; it has even less in it than the second."

"I don't know about that," Carl said. "Look at 'stun,' 'writhing,' 'dictates,' 'lash time'—that's a good one, and 'tore.' It all fits in with the Nazi torture theme."

"There's also 'arras,'" Evelyn said. "Hamlet stabbed Polonius behind the arras."

"But nothing new has been added," Karen pointed out.

"Why does there have to be anything new?" Jennifer asked.

"What would be the point of constructing a third puzzle," Bruce asked, "if the whole message was in the last two?"

"Pressure," Jennifer said. "Reinforcement. The more you bang away at Humboldt, the better. That way he can't ignore it. That's the only way to deal with these fascists."

"He's not ignoring it," Carl said. "He's just transferring the pressure to us. I'm not looking forward to Monday morning."

"Yeah," Evelyn said. "If two puzzles made him this sore, imagine what the third one will do."

"What more can he do to me?" Bruce asked bitterly. "If I don't get tenure, I might as well give up teaching altogether."

"Stop moaning and start thinking," Karen said. "Maybe our first analysis was wrong. Remember what Dag said the last time? About all the possibilities?"

"Mathematically speaking," Dag said, "the permutations of two hundred twenty-nine words taken in various lengths of statements will produce a very large number. However, themes which make sense and which make good English, and which use several words from each of the three puzzles, is a much smaller number, although still very large by any standard. Themes which might possibly be applied to our present situation, that would be a very small number, possibly only one—the one we have found."

"Let's study the puzzles some more," Karen said. "Try to put together a theme we can use."

They bent over their puzzles. After a few minutes Bruce said, "I tried all last night and I couldn't find a new theme. Most of the words are so innocuous you could use them in a children's book. Why don't we go back to the psych profile analysis?"

"Do you have anything new to add?" Carl asked.

"We didn't mention humor before," Bruce said. "There are several places in the puzzles where the clues are sort of funny, even witty. That's useful."

"So what do we know?" Karen asked. "The constructor is educated, familiar with some scientific terminology or at least knows where to look up the words, has some knowledge of common foreign words and mythology or, again, knows how to look them up, and he is intelligent and knows how to construct a crossword puzzle. He also has a sense of humor."

"You've just described every one of us," Bruce said.

"You've left out that he's Polish and wants revenge against the Nazis," Jennifer said.

"Zapata is eliminated from consideration," Bruce replied. "She doesn't fit two requirements—intelligence and humor."

"Stop that," Karen said. "Both of you." She took a deep breath. "We can't be sure the message we put together is the one that was intended, so any conclusions we draw from that message must be considered conjectural."

"According to Sherlock Holmes," Dag said, "when you have eliminated the impossible, what is left, no matter how improbable, is the truth."

"Except that we don't know what's impossible," Bruce said. "We're piling guess upon guess. That structure is not very stable."

"Why don't we just turn Humboldt over to the police?" Bruce asked.

"Are you crazy?" Evelyn exploded. "If he got so upset

over a couple of puzzles, what do you think he'll do to us over that?"

"And what do we charge him with?" Carl asked. "Imitating a professor? Can you imagine going to the cops with clues from a crossword?"

"Which we are not certain are correct?" Dag said.

"Have you really studied the puzzles, Bruce," Karen asked, "or just solved them?"

"Within the limits of the time available ... I'm pretty busy, you know."

"We don't seem to be doing much good here and now. Why don't you go to your office, Bruce, and study the puzzles very carefully? Why don't we all do that? We've got to have a solution by Monday morning or Humboldt will carry out his threat."

"I'll give you a solution right now," Carl said. "Stop Humboldt."

11

OLIVER WATCHED NERVOUSLY. "WHY IS MISS MACINtosh taking Mr. Giles into the forest?"

"Back of my property," Agatha Parrot said, "right there, see that opening between the trees? A footpath leads up to her cabin."

"It seems extremely narrow and uneven. Tortuous. And mountainous. How far is the cabin?"

"Under a mile as the crow flies, little over by foot. It's just a slight rise, not even a hill."

"The forest looks rather dark and thick. It's not the sort of place I would have thought Miss Macintosh would choose."

"Land was cheap, and there's no heavy traffic. It's a wood, not a forest. Windham Wood. Why do you have five big suitcases, Mr. Oliver?"

"Just Oliver will do. We are prepared for any contingency Mr. Giles may encounter, sartorially speaking. How am I to find my way to dress Mr. Giles this evening? Miss Macintosh departed so quickly, they left Mr. Giles's valises behind."

"He won't need any fancy dress this afternoon. I'll

lead you there later when Isabel calls me. Aren't you a butler, not a valet?"

"In a small household the distinction is, of necessity, blurred. Are you saying, Mrs. Parrot, that one must walk a mile uphill on that rude path in the dark, carrying two large, heavy valises?"

"Little over a mile, I said; the path winds a bit. If you're good at it—I am—and you know the way, you can ride a bike, if it has a powerful light. It's *Miss* Parrot; you can call me Agatha. Do you also do windows?"

"I supervise a professional cleaning crew that comes at regular intervals, Miss Parrot. Surely there is another way to get to Miss Macintosh's home. A taxi through the university grounds perhaps?"

"The main entrance is a couple of miles down this road, but they don't allow internal combustion engines on university property. And it's just as far through the wood from the edge of the campus to Isabel's cabin as it is from my back garden. I don't care what kind of Beau Brummel Mr. Sullivan is; he can't use up five suitcases of duds in two days."

"I will be bringing Mr. Giles only two of the valises. How then does the university have food, supplies, or mail delivered? Or furniture, equipment, and the like?"

"Hand trucks and hand trolleys. The air on campus smells sweet, even better than out here. Electric trucks for the big stuff. For people, shank's mare and bikes. Jogging. It's good exercise. The three big suitcases, they're for you?"

"Pants press, steamer, irons, similar necessities. My own personal effects, of course. Teapot and cozy. I need at least an hour to lay out Mr. Giles for Mrs. Jordan's reception tonight."

"We have to wait until Isabel calls. Plenty of time. Why don't you take a nap now? You'll need your strength tonight."

"An excellent idea. You will be sure to wake me on time?"

"No fear. I'll lend you a bike; we'll each take one suitcase on the bike rack. I never met a butler before, but, for sure, you don't have three suitcases full of cleaning fluid and brushes."

"There are requirements of my employment, Miss Parrot, tools of my trade you might say, of which you could not possibly be aware. In addition to the tools of my profession, Miss Parrot, I have books. On those rare occasions when I am away from Mr. Giles's town house, I read constantly. It is my only pleasure."

"You can always read when you get back to New York. As the Good Book says, man was not meant to be alone. Is Oliver your first name or your last?"

"It is my only name. And now, Miss Parrot, if you will show me to my room..."

"I'll bet if I looked it up, I'd find your full name. I'm good at finding things out, even if you haven't been able to do it yourself. Wouldn't you like that? You can call me Aggie."

"Mr. Giles would not approve of such liberties. Thank you, but I've already gone through the records quite thoroughly; I'd prefer if you didn't trouble."

"Isabel will speak to Mr. Sullivan and he'll *insist* you call me Aggie. I'll help you with the suitcases. My, this one is *heavy*. I'll leave it for you. You're sure you don't have a dead body in there or something?"

"Quite sure, Miss Parrot. Not that one either, please. If you insist, you may take any of the others. Will you open the front door for me, please? My hands are full."

"Nobody around here locks their doors; we're still in Vermont, you know. Can't say the same for New Hampshire, though. You're up the stairs to the right. Front bedroom. Right next to mine; just call out if you want anything. Bathroom's across the hall. You don't look it, Oliver, but you must be as strong as an ox, picking up those two suitcases at once. That can come in very handy, times."

"I endeavor to maintain good muscle tone. I do appreciate your hospitality, Miss Parrot."

"I'll bring you a hot potion tonight, Oliver, just before you're ready to go to sleep. Call me Agatha."

"Tea will do very well for me. Thank you. Agatha."

12

"**I** DON'T SEE PROFESSOR HUMBOLDT HERE," GILES SAID, looking around Mrs. Jordan's crowded entrance hall. "Do you?"

"I didn't know you knew what he looked like," Isabel said.

"I don't. All I know is that he's short, slim, and about my age. I remember reading about him somewhere."

"Humboldt never socializes. An hour for sherry for his students at his house at the beginning of each year fulfills his social obligations, in his mind. He lives like a monk; never even leaves the house as long as I've known him, except for school business."

"Isn't Mrs. Jordan offended by his refusal of her invitation? After all, Mr. Jordan is the president of Windham."

"She probably didn't even send him one—everyone knows how he is—although I'm sure he'd be welcome if he came; he's a very big name around here. No offense to Mavis Jordan was intended; if he ever decided to insult you, you'd know it loud and clear."

"How do you find him, Isabel? Difficult to work with?"

"Impossible. Not that he does much overtly disagreeable, just that he's so—so aloof. Thinks he's smarter than all the rest of us put together, which may or may not be true, but he could be a little less arrogant in either case."

"Do you know him well?"

"We nod at the Crossword Club, he's on the board, and he comes to my office occasionally to complain, but that's our only contact."

"You're dean of faculty. Doesn't he have to deal with you?"

"He doesn't have to do anything; he's a University Professor. Aggie and Virginia Wagner—she's his secretary—take care of all the routine arrangements."

"Aren't all professors university professors?"

"There's only one University Professor at Windham now, and there have never been more than two at any one time. A University Professor can teach any subject or subjects he wishes, or none at all, at any time, in any form. He can do any research, or none, as he wishes. He can use any university facilities he wishes for any purpose; no one can say him nay. Any graduate assistant, even an assistant professor, would drop everything if a University Professor offered to let him take part in whatever project the UP had in mind. It can be a shortcut to fame, fortune, or even a Nobel."

"I didn't realize Professor Humboldt was so important. Most people have never heard of him."

"In academic circles he's tops. Also in industrial and political circles; he's consulted all the time. He has an endowed chair with heavy funding from some big corporations. Windham needs him more than he needs Windham."

"What's he working on now?"

"Crosswords. He's had six assistant professors working like slaves for three years on a project having to do with crosswords, both solving and constructing. He also has a dozen graduate assistants working with the schools in Rockfield, teaching the kids how to solve crossword puzzles."

"And the school pays for all this? What is he doing it for?"

"The endowment pays for some of it. It doesn't quite come under the terms of the endowment, but we tend to give a University Professor a little leeway. Humboldt pays for the rest."

"Can he spend the endowment money any way he sees fit?"

"Certainly not. The school keeps firm control over the spending. If we let Humboldt have his way, he'd have a dozen projects going and half of Windham on his payroll. He's always fighting me to get more money, claims I'm blocking progress."

"If he really has that many good projects, why don't you release the money to him?"

"We budget for the whole school, not just for Fabian Humboldt."

"Doesn't he make extra money from his consulting work?"

"Practically all of it goes on his collections of weapons. Some of them are real antiques, and quite expensive. I don't think he has any money to spare. I'd really like to give him some more, but I can't do any better for him than I've already done. In fact, I've had lots of problems because I've tried to help him on his present project."

"Why should anyone object to his working on cross-words?"

"It isn't what he's working on, it's his way of just taking over everything, the people he uses. The department chairmen have bitched like crazy about their assistant professors working under Humboldt. It's most unusual for anyone to work outside his own department, but there's no way to stop them, if that's what they want to do. Why they do it is beyond me, although he's arranged to publish a scholarly book this year describing what his project is all about."

"Let me know when it comes out; I'll get a copy for the Cruciverbal Club library. You said before, he's even had six assistant professors helping him. Isn't that what an assistant professor is supposed to do?"

"If you knew more about how a university works... It's very unusual for assistant professors to work for anyone at all; they're too busy trying to get published. Humboldt not only has six; they're all from different departments. Not one is from his own department, history."

"Then why do they do it?"

"Hypnotism? Guaranteed tenure? Humboldt is highly respected and he serves on their tenure committees. It has to be something like that. After six years as an assistant professor, you're either granted tenure and made an associate professor or dropped. It all depends on your record of research and publication. And the quality of your scholarship, of course."

"Just dropped? No appeal? No recourse?"

"For all practical purposes, none. Unless the applicant is a protégé of a really powerful professor. Even then you have to show some publication. The ones who are not granted tenure have another year to try again—which is usually useless; nobody becomes a worthy scholar overnight—or to find another school where they may function better."

"That's sort of a life-or-death decision for them, isn't it? It must affect their whole professional careers. That's a cruel thing to do to a scholar."

"It's how to insure that you get real scholars in a university. I went through it; every one of us did. They knew it was publish or perish when they entered the profession. Most of them are mentally prepared to handle the situation. You mustn't think of scholars as being different from human beings; they really are human. They're fighters, Giles, not delicate flowers. You would be amazed at the intriguing, the infighting, the horse-trading, the struggle for dominance, that goes on in every department, not only by the candidates themselves but by the members of their tenure committees. It makes national politics look like potsy."

"Really? Everyone's been so nice to me tonight, so polite...."

"That's because you're not seen as a threat to anyone. If you were a rival..."

"But I am a rival—in one way at least. Hasn't any one of them ever coveted you? Lusted after you?"

"Not for years. To them I'm just a stiff old spinster. It's only you, Giles, who bring out the beast in me. Thank you for the lovely compliment."

"Your, uh, gown is very nice too, Isabel."

"Why don't you like it, Sullivan? Couldn't you have kept on the way you were going? Do you have to be so damned honest?"

"I said it was nice, really. It's just sort of—plain. Not like what you usually— It's, uh, black."

"*Elegant* is the word you were so desperately searching for, Sullivan. Women who wear black are supposed to be such striking beauties, they have no need of distracting plumage. *They* make the *gown* look beautiful." Giles started to protest, but Isabel put a finger to his lips. "Save your strength, darling. Leander swam the Hellespont just to be with Hero for an hour, and then swam back. But, of course, he was much younger than you. And more dashing. All I want from you is an occasional show of appreciation. You don't have to *do* anything, just say something romantic once in a while."

"I have asked you to marry me a hundred times, Isabel."

"Yeah, and you know how much romance I'd get after we were married? Pick a number smaller than zero."

"I did drop everything I had to do in New York just to come up here."

"Think of that; the wonder and the beauty of it all. For a whole big weekend. Who but Giles Sullivan would make that supreme sacrifice, O Prince among men?"

"Winston had scheduled—"

"And it took an invitation from the Crossword Club to

63

get you here, didn't it? So you could show off how smart you were. You couldn't think of coming up on your own, just to see me?"

"Isabel, did you arrange the lecture-demonstration for the benefit of the Crossword Club, or for your own pleasure?"

"I'm a member of the club, too, so the answer is yes. And my, aren't we gallant tonight? Cary Grant would have sworn that an invitation to share my cabin tonight was *entirely* to his benefit. The least you could have done tonight, Sullivan, was to drink that champagne from my slipper; I could use a little image-enhancement around here, especially now."

Giles was saved by Oliver's appearance at Isabel's elbow. "Would you like some refreshment, Miss Macintosh? Take this one. I made it myself just for you."

"It looks like a pousse-café, Oliver, but the colors are all wrong. What is it?"

"I named it in your honor: The Macintosh. One-quarter each of white crème de cacao and brown, one-sixth each of amaretto, vanilla extract, and heavy cream, all carefully floated in alternating light and dark layers."

"Oh, Oliver, you *do* really love me, don't you? Only you alone, of all men, would do something you despise to please me."

"The entire staff, Miss Macintosh, looks on you with favor. You will also be pleased to hear that all goes well with your program for Mr. Somerhill the Third."

"He's afloat in a fog of vodka?"

"I regret, madame, that your directions had some minor flaws, which I was forced to correct. Even an inexperienced person could detect the strength of unadulterated vodka, and might possibly choke on the potion and refuse to drink it down. I prepared, instead, a double-strength bloody Mary. The tomato juice, the Worcestershire sauce, and the Tabasco were enough to hide the faint flavor of certain extracts and infusions—only a few drops of each—which I added to facilitate the normal, truly laudable tendency to talk freely and openly. From the heart, so to speak."

"He isn't walking on the ceiling, is he?" Giles asked. "Or behaving in a highly uncharacteristic manner?"

"Not at all, sir. He is presently regaling a group of trustees and alumni with a detailed exposition of the novel techniques he intends to apply, when he becomes president, to the various problems he feels the university must solve."

"Do they fully understand his viewpoint, Oliver?" Isabel asked.

"Quite clearly, madame, in spite of a slight temporary speech impediment. They do not agree, however, that Mr. Somerhill's approach would have a beneficial effect on the quality of life or of learning at Windham. Quite the opposite, I would say."

"Good thinking, Oliver. Someday I will explain all. In the meantime, could I have another of those delicious eponymous . . . ?" Isabel placed the empty glass on Oliver's tray.

"I think I do understand, Miss Macintosh, and I approve wholeheartedly. I will be back as soon as I am able. It is difficult to walk smoothly in this crowd, and the slightest jar will mix the beautiful layers into a dull beige concoction."

"Wait a minute, Oliver," Giles said. "Did you leave your special valises, four and five, in Miss Parrot's house? Unguarded? Where anyone could, uh, steal them?"

"Have no fear, sir. I placed them under the bed. No respectable thief would think of looking for them there." Oliver turned away quickly, before Giles's face grew fully purple.

"Don't be such a fusspot, Giles," Isabel said. "There's no crime in Rockfield; not in a legal sense, anyway."

Suddenly the front door banged open. Virginia Wagner staggered into the entrance hall wearing a navy trench coat, her hair hanging in strands, tears and sweat streaming down her face. "He's dead!" she screamed. "They killed him!"

She fell to the floor in a faint. Her coat flew open, revealing a musical-comedy French maid's uniform, the tiny black skirt flipped up, plump white thighs shining between the sheer black stockingtops and the black lace panties. Her light-blue jogging shoes contrasted crazily with the sensual costume.

Isabel recognized the pattern of rosebuds sprinkled like drops of blood on the black garter-belt straps. We both patronize the same mail order house, Isabel thought numbly; sisters under the skin.

 **13** ✠✠✠

"**C**AN'T GO . . . IN HOUSE . . ." GILES SAID, STILL PANT-
ing. "Illegal. Entering. Trespassing."

"Nonsense," Isabel said. "Let go of my arm."

"First steal bikes. Ride to forest. Run up mountain.
Miles. No moon. Penlight. Could break neck. Now go in
house. Dead man. No. Wait for police."

"We'll give the bikes back later. We didn't run; we
jogged. A few hundred yards. I couldn't break my neck,
because I'm wearing low heels, thanks to Aggie. You can't
carry a big flashlight in an evening bag. So let's go in. It's
not illegal; the door's open."

"Can you imagine," Giles said, beginning to breathe
normally again, "what a sight we made? You with your
skirts tucked into your belt and me chasing you through
the forest? What would the neighbors have thought?"

"The headlines would have been—this is a college
town—'Satyr Pursues Nymph Through Windham Wood.
Nymph Guides Way with *Ignis Fatuus* and Waits Impatiently for Doddering Rake to Catch Up.' But no neighbors

would have seen us; there are only thirty cabins in the Wood, and they're all far apart."

"I am not doddering, just unused to clambering over rocks and roots in the dark. Do you mean to tell me that all those elegantly dressed ladies jogged or rode bikes to the Jordan party?"

"Of course not. The insiders did, and changed shoes in the bathrooms, but the outsiders came by car. Whenever there's a big affair, enterprising students run a rickshaw and pedicab service from the main gate."

"But how did you know where to go?"

"Everybody in the Wood knows where everybody else lives."

"I mean how did you know to come here? Who was that woman who ran into the entry hall? A prostitute?"

"Virginia Wagner? Are you kidding? She's his secretary. Since it wasn't Halloween, the costume— If she was fooling around with a townie, why would she run all the way to the Presidential Palace? Fathead's place is near the Wood, but quite far from the main gate. So it had to be him; he's always had an eye for the rounder types."

"Jealous? He never made a pass at you?"

"I let him know, early on, I don't go for intelligent men; I like joggers. And if you think I don't realize"— she twisted out of Giles's grasp—"that you're trying to keep me out here until the police come . . . But the police aren't coming yet. When we ran out I told Oliver to call Lou Quesada; he'll call the police. I'm going inside now. You want to stay out here with the bats, rats, and snakes in the dark, without me to protect you?"

"Don't touch the doorknob," Giles said. "Wait for me."

The tapping of Isabel's heels on the hard-waxed peggedpine floor echoed through the cabin. Isabel went directly to the dimly lit bedroom and pushed open the door. Empty.

"How'd you know where the bedroom is?" Giles whispered.

"A girl gets lonely, Sullivan, out here in the wilds." Isabel was marching rapidly along the corridor to the other spot of light. "So sometimes, at night, when the moon is full—" She stopped suddenly at the corner entrance of a long, dark, windowless room. "Oh. Oh, there he is."

From the doorway they could see dimly the three sides of the room, solid bookshelves from floor to ceiling, completely filled with books. In front of the long wall opposite them was a big wooden desk lit by a single low, green-shaded reading lamp hung from the ceiling. The cone of light it threw down showed neat piles of papers and several open books. The far corners of the room were in total blackness. Behind the desk was a small, slim, middle-aged man, leaning back in a big brown leather wing chair, supported in place by an oddly shaped sword about two feet long, with its guardless hilt resting on the desk and its broad, curved blade thrust horizontally between the dead man's ribs.

"Fabian Humboldt?" Giles whispered, then, loudly, "Isabel. Stay here."

"It's Humboldt, all right." Isabel had two fingers pressed to the side of Humboldt's neck. After a few seconds, "No pulse."

"Don't touch anything," Giles said, stepping carefully toward the desk.

"What is that thing?" Isabel asked, pointing to the short sword.

"I don't know," Giles said. "Looks Oriental to me, but usually curved swords have the sharp edge on the convex side of the blade; this one is sharp on the inside of the curve. And there's that rounded bulge, widening out of the blade, near the tip. That's also unusual. Let's get out of here. Fast."

"I thought you were an expert swordsman," Isabel said.

"I'm a fencer, not an expert on weapons. I can tell a foil from a sabre from an épée; that's about all. Where could that sword have come from?"

"Turn around," Isabel said. "That's where."

The long, dimly lit wall opposite Fabian Humboldt's desk was one huge pegboard completely covered with a variety of unlabeled weapons, all of them unfamiliar to Giles, lying loosely on brackets and hooks. Giles stared, fascinated, at the great display. "There must be a hundred swords and daggers here. More. I'd hate to be standing next to this wall in an earthquake. What is it for?"

"It's for his work," Isabel said. "I'll tell you about it later."

"Why are they loose? You could get killed just brushing up against that wall."

"Humboldt moves them—moved them around to form patterns that traced a path, showed lines of technological, industrial, and social progress. When he had a group set up properly, like a branching tree from left to right—similar to the evolutionary patterns in biology book illustrations—he would write, and later lecture, about the effect technological improvements derived from war had on human progress. There"—Isabel pointed to a pair of empty brackets about waist high, directly opposite Humboldt's desk—"there's where that thing came from."

"You're right," Giles said. "The killer must have taken it off the wall, stepped over—it's only one step—to Humboldt's desk, leaned across, and stabbed him."

"Sure," Isabel said, "but why did Humboldt just sit there?"

"What the hell are you two doing in there?" came a rough voice. "Get the hell out quick and don't touch anything. That goes for you too, Dean."

"What took you so long, Lou?" Isabel asked. "The killer could have had a facelift in Canada by the time you got here. Let me introduce Giles Sullivan, the eminent New York attorney, who is giving a lecture tomorrow at the Student Union. Giles, this is Lou Quesada, head of security at Windham."

Quesada's little black eyes took a series of identification shots of Giles from top to bottom. "What did you touch, Mr. Sullivan?"

"I touched his throat," Isabel said. "Other than that, nothing. Now that you're here, Lou, we'll leave."

"Wait outside the front door," Quesada said, taking a walkie-talkie out of his hip holster, "the police will want to talk to you."

 **14**

"**W**HAT ARE YOU TWO DOING HERE THIS LATE?" Isabel asked when she got back to her cabin.

"Oliver wanted to talk to Mr. Sullivan," Agatha said, "and I had a few things to discuss with you, Miss Macintosh."

"But it's two o'clock in the morning," Isabel protested. "The police kept us for hours. I should have been in bed hours ago."

"So should I," Agatha said, "by my calculations. If I can sacrifice for the good of the school, so can you."

"I'm afraid it was all my fault," Oliver said. "I just wanted to have a few words with Mr. Giles, if you don't mind. In private?"

"Sure," Agatha said, giving Isabel a look. "We'll just step outside. If it's okay with Miss Macintosh?"

Isabel nodded and Agatha closed the door firmly behind them. She walked about fifty feet uphill from the cabin before she spoke. "Just in case Oliver has his ear glued to a window," Agatha said. "I've got a feeling he's a lot smarter than he looks."

71

"I'm sure he is," Isabel agreed. "What's on your mind, Aggie? I'm really pooped."

"If you're really tired," Agatha said, "come sleep at my house; nothing much is going to go on there tonight, I'm afraid." She waited. Isabel looked up at the stars. "That's what I thought, Izzy. Don't play games with your old Aunt Aggie; I was smart while you were wetting your diapers." She paused a moment, then said, "Has Giles ever seen your black garter belt? The one with the rosettes?"

Isabel stared at her. "What has that got to do with...? No. I just bought it a month ago and decided to try it out at the cocktail party."

"Good. Don't wear it. Don't even show it to him. In fact, don't wear anything sexy this weekend; I don't want him to make the smallest mental connection between you and Virginia Wagner."

"But I had planned— Giles wouldn't do anything to hurt me, Aggie."

"He's a lawyer, isn't he? And a stuffed shirt, old-fashioned type, right? And what you told me about him and his brother? Strictly according to the law no matter what?"

"Not Giles..."

"Yes, Giles. Absolutely Giles. And he's a detective, too, isn't he? And didn't he almost kill the murderer in the Brundage case? Even though he liked him so much?"

"That was an accident. He wasn't trying—"

"Yeah, and he could accidentally tell the cops about your garter belt. That's why you can't show it to him."

"What has my garter belt...? You're jealous, Aggie. Just because your weekend is ruined, you're trying to spoil mine."

"Boy, when you've got the bit in your teeth, Izzy, you can't even see what's right in front of your nose. I'm beginning to wonder what kind of president you'd make for Windham, unless, of course, you got married and gave up sex. What do you think the papers will say tomorrow?"

"'Professor Murdered with Own Sword'?"

"Wrong! 'Secretary's Sex Tryst Uncovers Murder.' How do you like them apples?"

"Oh. I see. It could lead—"

"It sure could. Not the police, but some reporter, is going to con our Virgie into talking too much, or sneak into her house and go through her closets, then her bills, and in one hour he'll know who she's been buying from. You don't think she's been wearing that one costume all these years, do you? French maids are fine, but not for a steady diet."

"I'm sure Humboldt demanded variety. That was the purpose of the costume, to provide the variety of appearance for people like Virginia who aren't sufficiently innovative to—" She stopped suddenly.

"I can't believe that's why— You should have come to your Aunt Agatha. I would have taught you the secrets of the inscrutable missionary position," Agatha said sarcastically. "Relax, Izzy. I know better. I'm sure it was just curiosity, to see what it would be like. I've done it myself. Nothing wrong with a little change of scene now and then as long as it doesn't become a habit. But let's stop philosophizing and get back to business. Now, what's the next step for our enterprising young reporter?"

"If he can, he gets the customer list from the plain-brown-wrapper mail order house and checks for our zip code. Windham U. or Rockfield."

"In any organization there's always someone bribable. And when our reporter finds the name of Isabel Macintosh, Dean of Faculty, and what's worse, one more name, anybody living within ten miles of Rockfield—you two are not the only explorers of the unendurable ecstasy in this neck of the woods—what will the headlines say?"

"'Sex Orgies Uncovered at Windham University. What Really Goes On Behind Ivy-Covered Walls. What Are They Teaching Your Children?'"

"I think you've got it."

"I'm going to burn my garter belt."

"Too late. Everybody knows you've got it."

"Then what can I do, Aggie?"

"Tomorrow's Sunday, or rather, today. It'll be at least three days before anybody can trace anything back to you, maybe more. It was an out-of-state place, wasn't it?" Isabel nodded. "Good. Tomorrow they'll all be concentrating on the murder; the sex thing will be a side issue. By Wednesday the reporters will be searching for ways to keep the story alive. That's our deadline."

"Deadline for what?"

"Why, to find the murderer, of course."

15

"I WAS JUST THINKING," AGATHA SAID, "THIS MURDER of Professor Humboldt—he was a highly respected scholar, you know. Held the rank of University Professor. Very few professors ever reach that title."

"So I understand," Giles said. "I know very little about his field, but even I have heard the name."

"The newspapers are sure to have a field day," Isabel said. "Who knows what they could report?"

"Yes," Agatha said, "they'd make Windham University sound like Bennington."

"That's an in joke," Isabel explained. "Around here Bennington is—we're rivals, you know—Bennington is shorthand for anything you fear and dislike: witchcraft, football, mercantilism. . . . Actually Bennington isn't all that bad. In some ways."

"The point is," Agatha continued, "we've had a murder on campus, or just off. As far as the papers are concerned, and the television, Professor Humboldt was killed in the middle of a lecture by a crazed administrator."

"Well, what can we do about it?" Isabel asked. "How can we save our reputation?"

"If I might be so bold, Madame," Oliver said, "possibly you could persuade Mr. Giles to look into the matter? He has had a great deal of experience with the criminal law, and solved one case recently that baffled the police."

"That's a great idea," Agatha said. "What do you think, Miss Macintosh?"

"I'm afraid," Isabel said with a sideways glance at Giles, "that Mr. Sullivan hadn't planned on working during his very short vacation."

"Ah, well," Giles said, "I'm sure I can spare a little time. Duty, you know. For the sake of the university."

"But what about all those important duties you tore yourself away from in New York?" Isabel said. "Don't you have some major obligations there too?"

"I'm sure they will understand," Oliver said, "that Mr. Giles feels that his responsibility here—inasmuch as he and Miss Macintosh surveyed the scene of the crime jointly—must take precedence over ordinary business matters."

"But it may take some time," Agatha said, "to solve the case. Maybe as long as . . . until Wednesday night. Can Mr. Sullivan be gone that long?"

"With your permission, Mr. Giles," Oliver said, "I will phone Mr. Winston and ask him if he could possibly postpone the consultation until late Thursday. Or Friday morning. I'm sure he will understand."

"If you're not going to be in Winston's office until Friday morning," Isabel said, "why not skip Friday, too, and stay here next weekend? You'll be busy until Wednesday, so that won't be very restful for you."

"We'll have to postpone today's lecture too," Agatha said, "till next Sunday, out of respect to Professor Humboldt. I'll arrange it."

"Well, I—uh, yes, I suppose that would be all right," Giles said. "I'll call Henry Winston and explain it to him. There may be a few other little things I can look into at the same time."

"That's just great, Mr. Sullivan," Agatha said. "But I

still think it's very important that the case be closed by Wednesday. The longer it drags, the greater the damage. To Windham University."

"I would agree with Miss Parrot," Oliver said. "Wednesday at the outside."

"Now, see here," Giles said. "You can't tell me I must solve this case by a certain date. I don't know anything about it."

"Of course you can," Isabel cooed. "You solved the Brundage case in much less time, and there you didn't even know *how* the murder was done. I would love for you to have a *real* vacation from Thursday—from Wednesday night on."

"And I'll help," Agatha said. "Just tell me what to do."

"It seems to me," Oliver said, "that it would be useful to speak with Mrs. Wagner. Can you arrange that, Miss Parrot?"

"I'll talk to her in words of one syllable," Agatha said grimly. "She'll be at your office, Miss Macintosh, at eight o'clock tomorrow morning. *This* morning."

"Eight o'clock?" Isabel was aghast. "On Sunday morning? I never get out of bed until—"

"We all have to make some sacrifices, don't we?" Agatha said with a sincere-looking smile. "But in the service of a higher righteousness, I'll make it nine."

#################### 16 ####

"**W**HAT WILL HAPPEN TO ME NOW?" VIRGINIA WAG-
ner's eyes were red, her face puffy from lack of sleep.
She sat opposite Isabel's desk in the hard wooden chair
Agatha Parrot had provided.

"That depends on many things," Isabel said. "You realize, of course, with Professor Humboldt gone there may
be no place for you here."

"But I need the job, Miss Macintosh. My father—"

"You haven't exactly endeared yourself to others at
the university, Virginia. It will be very hard to place you."

"Miss Parrot said, if I helped you"—she glanced sideways at Agatha—"that you would take care of me."

"If you cooperate, Virginia, I'll do what I can. Tell me
how you came to find Professor Humboldt last night."

Virginia Wagner wet her lips and looked from side to
side. "I—every Saturday night I had to go—be there. At
exactly ten o'clock. He liked everything punctual."

"What time did you leave your house?"

"About ten to. It's not far; his house is the first one

you come to on that path, but I had to go around, not on the paths people usually used."

"You jogged?"

"He didn't want me to use my light, so I had to walk. Besides, it would look funny to jog in a hat and coat if anyone did see me, accidentally."

"You weren't wearing a hat when you got to President Jordan's house."

"It must have come off when I was running. I was scared."

"Running in the wood without a light?"

"Everybody has a light; I just couldn't use it going there."

"Did you see anyone in the wood that night, Virginia? Did anyone see you?"

"Nobody. His house is sort of off by itself. Going down the hill to the campus, I didn't see anyone either. I don't know if anyone saw me."

"How long had this affair been going on, Virginia?"

"Is Agatha taking notes? The police told me not to say anything to anybody."

"You're not nailed to the chair, Virgie," Agatha said. "There's the door."

Virginia Wagner crumpled. "I—it's been three years. After my husband died I was—he—it just happened."

"Your husband died four years ago, Virgie," Agatha said. "In all that time, for a whole year, he never made a pass at you? Or before that?"

Virginia Wagner pursed her lips disapprovingly. "Professor Humboldt would never even think...he had very strict standards...with a married woman. He told me later that he waited for me for a year before—he was very proper. Very."

"Did he ever mention marriage to you?"

"He wasn't the marrying kind; everybody knew that. He lived for his work."

"You said you had to go to Humboldt's house. Did he threaten you?"

"It was nothing like that at all. It was just...understood. I was all alone...lonely...I wouldn't like, with a married man . . . it's such a small town—people talk. I had to stay here; my father needed me. He would never come to my house."

"What about the costumes? There were several, were there not?"

"He gave me the money and had me buy them. I had to pick which one to wear according to my mood. There's nothing wrong with dressing up, playacting. It was fun, sometimes. I carried the shoes in my bag."

"You always walked?"

"It's dangerous to jog in the dark. I had plenty of time. Usually I got there a little early. I didn't want to get all sweated up."

"Did anyone ever see you go there?"

"Never. I'm sure of it. He was very concerned about that. If he thought anyone knew, he might even have fired me."

"After ten years of loyal service," Agatha said, "and three years of—romance?"

"He liked things—regular. A place for everything and everything in its place."

"Did you notice anything different," Isabel asked, "when you got there that night?"

"As soon as I opened the door I knew something was wrong. Usually only the bedroom light was on, but I could see, down the hall, that there was a light on in the study. He would never do that, so instead of locking the door behind me, as I usually did, I went—in there."

"You had a key?"

"He used to leave the front door unlocked for me while he waited in the bedrom. But he wasn't—he was in the study. There he was—he didn't move. I knew he was dead; I just knew. So I ran out. I didn't know what to do."

"Why did you go to President Jordan's house?"

"He was the nearest. I had to tell someone. What else could I do? If they found out I was there and didn't tell them, they'd think I did it."

"Did you, Virginia?"

"How can you say that, Miss Macintosh? You know I

couldn't do—why should I? I've lost everything." She burst into tears.

"All right, Mrs. Wagner," Isabel said, "I believe you. I'll see what I can do. Go home and get some sleep; I may want to talk to you again tomorrow, and I'd like you to be relaxed when I do. Please don't tell anyone, not even the police, that you spoke to me." As the door closed behind Virginia Wagner, Isabel said, "Take her home, Aggie. Give her a tranquilizer."

"Sure. Meet you at your house in half an hour. Is Mr. Sullivan up yet?"

"He will be by the time you get back. Why?"

"We should plan things, not do deep knee bends. Four heads are better than two."

"Oliver?"

"He's no fool, that one. We had a talk on the way home last night."

"You didn't use Grandpa's special elixir?"

"It wasn't the right time. But on Wednesday night . . ."

"You have a lot of faith in Sullivan, Aggie."

"There's nothing like necessity to stir up the brain cells, Izzy. If we don't produce by Wednesday, we might as well close up shop for good."

17

"THAT'S GOOD COFFEE, OLIVER," AGATHA SAID. "How'd you like to cook for me regular?"

"I'm afraid," Oliver said, "that my repertoire is extremely limited. Would anyone like more waffles? The maple syrup is excellent."

"It's worth your life, in Vermont," Agatha said, "to say any different. Why don't you sit down too, Oliver? We need all the help we can get."

"I'm afraid it would not be seemly. With Mr. Giles's permission, I will join you if I have anything to add. It might be useful if you were to brief Mr. Giles on Professor Humboldt's background."

"I know even more about him than Miss Macintosh does," Agatha said. "He's been here ever since he got out of school. Brilliant student, everyone predicted great things for him. If he'd gone to one of the big-name schools, who knows where he might be by now. Guess he was happy here, or else he liked being a big frog in a little puddle."

"Did he have a family, Agatha?" Giles asked.

"Not that anyone knew of, Mr. Sullivan. Always been a loner. No friends either, although there's been rumors, now and then, about him and some of the graduate students."

"If there was anything going on with graduate students," Isabel said, "he handled it very discreetly. The only gossip I had heard was some whispers about him and Virginia Wagner."

"Never any real evidence, though, about grads or Wagner," Agatha said. "Otherwise I would have told you. He had some mighty big connections in Washington; that I've heard for sure."

"He was often consulted," Isabel said, "but not just by government officials. His chair was endowed by a private corporation."

"A front for the CIA," Agatha said firmly.

"Are you sure?" Giles asked.

"Can't prove it," Agatha said. "But I have my suspicions."

"Do you think his death was, uh, political?" Giles asked. "The KGB or some similar organization?"

"That sounds promising," Isabel said eagerly. "Why don't I—we call some people we know in Washington and ask them to find out?"

"The circumstances are such," Oliver said smoothly, "as to preclude any possibility of its being political. Don't you agree, Miss Parrot?"

"The way Miss Macintosh described the scene," Agatha said, "it looks more like a crime of passion."

"Virginia Wagner?" Isabel said doubtfully. "I don't see her as capable of it; she was too much under his control."

"Worms turn," Agatha said. "Still waters run deep. But it wasn't Virgie, couldn't be. And there's passions and passions. Life's not all sex and jealousy, you know."

"What else?" Isabel asked. "Money?"

"Fear, hate, greed, envy—there's lots of passions. Didn't you read the books, Miss Macintosh, that you used to teach?"

"Miss Parrot is right," Oliver said. "It might be useful to look into other motivation."

"But no one can possibly gain by Humboldt's death," Isabel said.

"As far as we know, Miss Isabel," Oliver said, "and we should look into that more deeply. But possibly the reverse?"

"Who loses if he lives?" Giles mused. "That's a good point, Oliver. What do you know about that, Isabel?"

"I can't imagine anyone—unless he was blackmailing somebody. Did you ever hear anything like that, Aggie?"

"Nope, Humboldt wasn't the type. Didn't need to use blackmail; he bulldozed people. Direct talk, direct action; that was his way. I don't mean he was a nice guy, but he did have a code."

"Then what could be the motive?" Giles asked. "Why would anyone kill him?"

"Should we not examine the sexual angle more closely?" Oliver suggested. "Tracing the source of Mrs. Wagner's costume might prove rewarding."

"Oh, I don't think that will produce anything useful," Agatha said. "If there was a sex cult, or anything like that around here, I would have known about it. What about the murder weapon, Mr. Sullivan? You said it was very unusual."

"It was," Giles said. "I'd been meaning to ask Oliver about that. Get me a piece of paper, Isabel, and a pencil." Isabel put a legal pad on the table. "The sword was about two feet long, Oliver, with a grip-shaped haft. No guard. The blade had a sort of odd bend, about thirty degrees, near the handle, and a slight convex curve on the outside. Sort of like a scimitar, but not nearly as round. The inside of the curve was sharp, and it also had a somewhat convex widening out near the tip. I'm sure it had a sharp point, although the tip was buried in Humboldt's chest."

"Was the blade thick and heavy?" Oliver asked. "And did it have a notch on the inside, near the handle? Like this?" Oliver took the pencil and corrected the drawing.

"That's it, Oliver." Giles was excited. "You know what it is?"

"It's a Gurkha knife, sir," Oliver said. "The Gurkhas all carried them, the Indian soldiers, you know. From Nepal. Very fierce fighters, I am told."

"Indian?" Giles was puzzled. "Did Professor Humboldt have any connection with India?"

"Not that I ever heard of," Agatha said.

"I don't think it was anything like that," Isabel said. "It was more like—the sword was at a convenient place— just happened to be at waist height opposite the desk. Any other weapon that was there would have been used."

"Are you saying this was an unplanned murder?" Giles asked. "Spur of the moment?"

"That is possible," Oliver said, "but there is also the possibility that the killer knew that the sword, or *a* sword, would be available in that study if he decided to kill the professor. But the question remains, sir, how did he know Professor Humboldt would invite him into the study?"

"It was obviously someone who knew Professor Humboldt," Giles said. "Anyone could have gotten in through the unlocked front door, the one Isabel told me was left unlocked for his mistress, Mrs. Wagner. But if it was someone Humboldt didn't know, he wouldn't have been sitting behind his desk; he would have grabbed a sword himself and attacked the intruder. Wouldn't he?"

"No doubt about it," Agatha said. "He was a mean-tempered little bastard; got very sore if anyone interfered with his plans. No, he knew the killer all right. In fact, he must have been in the bedroom waiting for Virginia Wagner when the killer came in and said, 'Anyone home?' or whatever. Then Humboldt invited the killer into the study for a few words."

"That makes sense," Isabel said. "But with Virginia on the way, he was probably telling the killer to state his business and get the hell out."

"Then why in the study?" Giles asked. "Why not in the hall?"

"Because it was almost time for Virginia to arrive," Agatha said. "She would normally have gone right into the bedroom. Humboldt didn't want the killer to see her, so he was going to keep the killer in the study until he heard Virgie arrive, and then let the killer out. That way, neither would see the other one."

"Why didn't Humboldt throw the killer out right away?" Giles asked.

"The killer might have met Virginia on the path," Isabel said, "and the affair would have become public knowledge."

"Agatha," Giles asked, "could you use your resources to find the exact time of death from the police?"

"I already know that," Agatha said. "Between nine-forty-five and ten. Humboldt was one of the few people around here who lock their doors. Knowing him, he didn't unlock the front door before nine-forty-five."

"Could the killer have gotten a key?" Giles asked. "Maybe from Humboldt himself? Or made a copy?"

"If Virginia didn't have a key," Agatha said, "no one did."

"What you're saying," Giles said, "is that the killer knew Professor Humboldt well enough to come uninvited and not get thrown out right away, but not well enough to know about Mrs. Wagner's Saturday-night visits." He leaned toward Isabel. "Does that put you in mind of anyone?"

"No one," Isabel said at once. "I not only don't know of anyone like that, I can't believe there is such a person. Humboldt would have a fit if you accidentally walked into his *office* without an appointment."

"How did the killer know the front door was unlocked at that time?" Giles asked. "Neither Mrs. Wagner nor Professor Humboldt would have told him, I'm sure."

"Maybe he didn't," Agatha said. "Maybe he just walked up and knocked and Humboldt let him in. Although that doesn't sound like the Fabian Humboldt I know."

"Normally," Isabel said, "Humboldt would have let the visitor knock until he was blue in the face, even in the daytime, or else called the police, but with Virginia coming any minute, he might have let the killer in to avoid his meeting the new French Maid."

"That doesn't sound right," Giles said. "The visitor knows where Humboldt's house is and can find it at night.

He knows Humboldt well enough to be invited in, into the study, and to talk with Humboldt for long enough so that Humboldt would sit down behind his desk, even though Mrs. Wagner is due any minute. If the visitor came before Humboldt unlocked the door for Mrs. Wagner, either Humboldt had made an appointment for that time, which is crazy, or the visitor had just phoned Humboldt and told him the matter was of such urgency—"

"Scratch that, Giles," Isabel said. "Humboldt didn't have a phone in the house."

"Could the visitor have come unannounced?" Oliver asked. "When Professor Humboldt wouldn't answer the bell, the visitor tried the door and found it unlocked."

"That's stretching coincidence too far," Agatha said. "Anyone Humboldt knew well enough to invite in wouldn't come visiting without an invitation, and he wouldn't have gotten an invitation from Humboldt, especially for that time. But isn't it possible that Humboldt was killed at nine? Or earlier?"

"No," Giles said. "He was killed just before ten. When Isabel and I saw him the blood was still wet. If you find out anything different from the police, let me know."

"It may be," Oliver said, "that the killer had no intention of becoming a killer when he decided to visit Professor Humboldt. That would explain the impromptu use of the Gurkha knife from the weapons wall."

"It's also possible," Giles said, "that he did bring a weapon with him and took the sword from the wall to avoid leaving a possible means of identification behind."

"If the killer had come armed," Agatha said, "he would have picked a weapon small enough to hide in his clothes, so he could have taken it away with him easily."

"And why," Isabel asked, "if someone who hated Humboldt enough to kill him came unexpectedly into the house, did Humboldt sit quietly in his chair and let himself be killed? And with such a clumsy weapon?"

"Possibly," Oliver said, "the intruder had a gun and forced Professor Humboldt to sit in the study while he killed him with the sword."

"Whatever for?" Giles asked. "Just to confuse us?"

"That is a possibility, sir," Oliver said. "Or we may discover another reason as we delve more deeply."

"We must find out more about Humboldt's various enterprises," Giles said. "We're working with insufficient information, making inferences from assumptions piled on surmise, unable to answer definitely even the simplest questions."

"Virginia Wagner," Agatha said. "She handled all of Humboldt's correspondence, in and out. She knows more about him than anyone else in the world does. Let's get her."

"But we spoke to her just two hours ago," Isabel objected. "She's had no sleep, practically, all night. Can't we let her rest awhile?"

"I'll give her another hour," Agatha said, looking at her watch, "then you and Mr. Sullivan go to her house and find out what you want to know."

"It's really too much, Aggie," Isabel said.

"Didn't we agree Mr. Sullivan had to find the killer by Wednesday?" Agatha looked at Isabel fiercely. "Besides, you can tell Virgie she's got a job, if she cooperates. Definitely."

"A job? Where, Aggie?"

"After Wednesday, when Mr. Sullivan finds the murderer, we're going to be very, very busy. On the new campaign, you know. I'm going to need an assistant to take care of the routine work. Virgie's a good secretary; you have enough clout to clear it with Personnel. I wouldn't mind having her helping me, long as she knows her place."

18

"**B**UT I'VE ALREADY TOLD YOU EVERYTHING." VIR-
ginia Wagner pulled her worn terry-cloth bathrobe tightly
around her plump body. How different, Isabel thought,
from the French Maid's garter belt. And mine. We take
our roles, live our parts, each in turn, if we believe, truly
believe, want pathetically to believe, that we are what
our costumes create. And more—we want to be believed
in. Like Tinker Bell.

And I, even I—a teacher of literature, I know what I
am—playing dean, playing detective. Without even a
magnifying glass to sustain the illusion. But if I don't tell,
maybe Giles won't find out. Or Virginia Wagner.

"I'm so tired," Virginia said. "So tired. The police kept
me up till three."

"Just a few more questions," Isabel said.

Virginia sighed and glanced up the stairs. "But please
keep your voice down; he's still sleeping."

"Did you have any—was there anyone, Virginia, who
might have been jealous of Professor Humboldt?"

"They were all—oh, you mean about me?" She colored slightly. "Certainly not. I never— My husband and I were married right after high school. He was the only— I was a good wife to him."

"And after his death? There was a year, you said?"

"I didn't feel—all I could think of was to keep body and soul together. I had responsibilities."

"Until Professor Humboldt, um, declared his love?"

Virginia shook her head tiredly. "It wasn't love, Miss Macintosh. Not for me, and certainly not for him. Who could love...? I'm too old for that kind of nonsense. But it was nice, exciting even. It made me feel— Everybody, even if it's just once a... Now I have nothing."

"I'm sure you'll—" Isabel did not want to go on, especially with Giles next to her. She and Virginia Wagner, like most women, had more in common than garter belts. And Virginia was ten years younger. Fortunately men didn't understand, especially Giles. Or unfortunately. "Was there anyone who was jealous of you, Virginia?"

"Of me?" The thought clearly had never crossed her mind. "Who would...? There were always the students, especially the graduate assistants, who would have liked— with an older man—a really great man— But they wouldn't be jealous of me, the young girls; their minds would go flitting around, like butterflies, not really thinking. If the professor ever gave any one of them a sign—maybe. But he never did. To him, a student... You just didn't, with students. He was a gentleman of the old school. Besides, no one knew; I was just the secretary."

It was time to change direction, Isabel felt. "What was Professor Humboldt working on before he was killed?"

"He had two projects: one for the navy, one for the air force. The short-term effects of using flexible chains of spherical soft-plastic containers towed by tractor ships to transport oil, and the other on the long-term effects of a trapezoidal array of four large stable platforms in fixed orbit. And the Project, of course."

"Was either of the military applications secret?"

"I'm sure they weren't. There are clippings in the files from newspapers and magazines."

"I've heard a little of the Project, Virginia. Tell me the details."

"I'm not sure I should, Miss Macintosh. Everything was supposed to be kept secret."

"Professor Humboldt is dead," Isabel reminded her gently.

"Yes. I'm sorry." Virginia seemed confused. "It's just that— We called it the Project because we didn't want others to know what we were doing. He had other projects, when he was younger—lots of things he first thought of were stolen and others got the credit. It was called the Crossword Project. The idea was . . . students today . . . the professor was very upset, angry, that children, students, didn't read anymore. They had television, movies, computer games, headphones they listened to all the time. He wanted them to read, to think. If he gave them games, real games, for pleasure, things they enjoyed which involved reading . . . They'd learn to read and to think without ever knowing they were learning."

"That sounds reasonable. Why the big secret?"

"You can't just— He had lots of data, Miss Macintosh. Fully correlated. Learning curves and everything. We had been trying it out in the Rockfield schools for three years. It was very successful. We were getting ready to publish a scholarly book; in fact, he had also begun dickering with another publisher, a big one, a few weeks ago. The Project would have had a great influence on education. We were going to apply for next year's Liberman Prize."

"What's the Liberman Prize?" Giles asked.

"It's put out by a group of book clubs," Isabel said. "Goes to the one who has done the most to promote reading."

"It's a great honor," Virginia said. "I think the Project would have won."

"Was that why he was so secretive about the Project?" Giles asked.

"You'd be surprised how people are in the academic world, Mr. Sullivan. They're always sneaking around, trying to find out what you're doing so they can steal it, especially from a genius like Professor Humboldt."

"Even so," Isabel said, "but the emphasis on secrecy seems excessive to me. Was this a result of his military orientation?"

"Maybe, I suppose, Miss Macintosh, but I think he was right. There was the chance that somebody would catch on to what he was doing, somebody from a big university with lots of funds, who could whip up a flashy copy of the Project and take the Liberman Prize from us. That was very important to the professor; he was counting on the publicity to help him get the funds for all the other projects he had in mind."

"Was that all there was to the Project, Virginia? Just teaching reading?"

"Well, if you're learning reading, Miss Macintosh, you're also learning writing, spelling, grammar, punctuation—all these things. We didn't just have English and education; we also had psychology and sociology to make sure that what was learned was appropriate, and fitted the other things the children learned in school. We had third world studies, too, to make sure the puzzles fitted the minority kids; they really needed help the most. It was a really comprehensive setup."

"How could Professor Humboldt handle all this," Giles asked, "if he had two other major projects going at the same time? His private projects?"

"He had some graduate assistants doing the research. As for the Project, Dr. Karas took care of all the routine arrangements. By this time the procedures were established and each of the junior professors did his special work almost automatically. Dr. Karas organized the reports and the solving sessions, and I did the typing and filing."

"Did any outsiders know any of the details of the Project?"

"That's impossible," she said flatly. "Of course, everyone knew what the Project was, more or less, and that we were working on it, but not the details. The professor was very insistent on privacy; I kept all the correspondence that was on my desk one on top of the other with only the letterheads showing so the visitors couldn't read anything upside down."

"Did you read all his mail, Virginia?"

"Everything. Mail, phone calls, everything."

"Was there anything unusual in the past few weeks? Or months?"

"Not what I would consider—unless you mean the seventh crossword. Crosswords. It didn't seem like so much to me, but the professor was really put out."

"What seventh crossword?"

"In the past week— There are the six teachers, assistant professors—they're not tenured yet—who have been working on the Project. They make up crosswords that they solve themselves three times a week, and test them out on the schoolchildren. In the past week somebody's been putting a seventh puzzle in with the others. Three times. After the first time the professor called in Karen and gave her hell about it."

"Why her?"

"She's supposed to keep things running right. Last Friday—my God, that was just two days ago; so much has happened—last Friday, after the second puzzle, the professor called all six in and told them they'd better get to the bottom of this or else he'd drop the whole Project. Without him, well, everything would go to waste. Also they'd probably none of them get tenure. They were real upset, I can tell you. I mean, it was like the end of the world."

"Over three extra crossword puzzles?" Isabel couldn't believe this.

"You have no idea, Miss Macintosh. I've been with him for ten years now, and I've never seen him so angry. He was just about ready to kill somebody, if only he knew who."

"May I ask a few questions?" Giles said. "Did you see these puzzles, Mrs. Wagner?"

"Of course. I see everything and I file everything."

"Was there anything different about them?"

"They were just like the others, far as I could see. Only

there was no name and no code number for the grade and difficulty level."

"Did any of the six, or Professor Humboldt, say anything about the puzzles? Form or content?"

"The professor said that the constructor of the puzzles was out to destroy the Project."

"The Project? Not Professor Humboldt?"

"That's the way I remember it; I could check my notes."

"Please do and let me know if you find any difference. You say Professor Humboldt threatened to stop the Project over these three additional puzzles?"

"There were only two at the time. The third came in late that afternoon."

"You gave it to Professor Humboldt?"

"Right away. He closed the door, to solve it I guess. He always had to solve a puzzle right away. When he came out he was boiling."

"Will you give me a copy of the puzzles, please?"

"I'll go to the office later and drop them through the dean's mail slot. I can only get you the blanks, though; if he solved them, he kept the answers to himself."

"That's all right," Giles said. "I can solve them if I have to. Did Professor Humboldt threaten anyone else to your knowledge? Other than the six assistant professors, I mean."

"Nobody else. He didn't threaten them either, just told them what he'd do if they didn't find out who made up those puzzles."

"Did anyone ever threaten Professor Humboldt?"

"Sure. All six of them, each in their own way. If looks could kill, the professor would have been dead right then and there."

19

"**L**ET'S PUT TOGETHER WHAT WE KNOW ABOUT THE killer so far," Giles said.

"Let's have lunch first," Agatha said. "Oliver and I put together what little we could find."

"I wasn't expecting guests," Isabel said. "If you'll give me a few minutes to run down to town—"

"Why don't we talk while we eat?" Giles said. "That way we won't notice starvation setting in." There was no riposte from Isabel. "Why are you so quiet?" Giles asked. "I was only kidding."

"I was just thinking," Isabel said, "about what Virginia Wagner told us. The only threats to Humboldt were from the six assistant professors working on the project. It would be terrible for the school if one of them did it. I was hoping so it was an outsider, the KGB or the PLO or something like that."

"If it was an organization like that," Giles said, "you would never be able to prove anything in an American court of law. Look at the attempted assassination of the Pope."

"I really don't care," Isabel said, "if we never prove anything. I mean, I'd like justice done and all that, but I'm more concerned that the university isn't involved. It's bad enough that Humboldt was murdered; think how it would look if another professor did it."

"Are you suggesting that we stop trying, Isabel?" Giles asked.

"No, not really. We have to find the killer. I was just hoping it isn't one of ours."

"What's the probability that one of those six is involved?" Giles asked.

"Very low. They're all nice kids—kids, listen to me. Shows how old I feel. They're all assistant professors, good teachers, hard workers. Even Zapata, who's a big pain."

"Zapata? A descendant of the great Mexican revolutionary?"

"I think not, though she acts as though she is. Her father's one of the biggest produce merchants in the Southwest and a heavy donor to the university."

"You know them all?"

"Of course. Professionally, that is." Isabel put her hand on Giles's arm. "I'd really hate to see any of them—"

"Are you trying to exert undue influence on me to . . . ?"

"I guess I am, but not really. You wouldn't let me. . . ." She looked into his eyes. "I guess not. I don't even know if I'd want you to." Isabel paused, then said, "Do your best, Giles. I'll help."

"Isabel"—Giles hesitated—"Isabel, if it's a faculty member or an administrator who is the killer, I'll have to turn him over to the police."

"I said I'd help you," Isabel said sharply. Oliver and Agatha put the *salade Niçoise* on the table. They all filled their plates.

"I think I should speak to the six professors in Humboldt's crossword Project," Giles said. "Can you arrange it?"

"Easily, if they're around," Isabel said. "Anyone who

is close to tenure, and especially someone who is up for tenure this year, will jump through hoops for me, for anyone who could have the slightest influence on his tenure committee."

"Let's talk to them as quickly as possible," Giles said. "I'm sure there's more to the Project than Mrs. Wagner saw. I'd like to know what it was about the extra crosswords that angered Humboldt. It could lead us to more fertile fields."

"I have a feeling, Giles, you want to show off how good you are at crosswords, but why not? Aggie, will you find out who's home and make appointments for us to go to each one right after lunch? Set them about an hour apart, and try to arrange the least possible walking."

"All of them?" Giles asked. "Six in one day?"

"The time to talk to them is now, before the police get to them. Right now the police don't even know they exist, that they have a connection to the murder."

"We don't know that either, Isabel."

"They have a connection, Mr. Sullivan," Agatha said. "I have a feeling."

"What if they're not at home, Miss Parrot?"

"They're home, all right." Agatha said. "Where else can an assistant professor go on his salary?" Agatha went to the phone and started dialing. Although he wasn't listening, Giles noted that the calls were short. Agatha wasn't asking; she was telling.

When Agatha returned, Giles said, "Let's organize what we know about the killer. We'll start with his arrival at Humboldt's house."

"We have to go back further," Agatha said. "We're all agreed that he knew the professor, because Humboldt took him into his study and sat down to talk to him."

"And he knew the way to Humboldt's cabin," Isabel said. "Whether you're coming from the campus or from the town streets, you have to know your way through the wood."

"Has to be from the town," Agatha said. "If there's the slightest possibility you're going to kill Humboldt, you'd be a damn fool to go through the campus, where anyone could see you; the campus is a lot better lit than the town."

"I'll accept that," Giles said. "Any idea which part of town?"

"Any part," Isabel said. "With a bike you can get across town in a few minutes. And if you know your way around the wood, you can start from anywhere and get to anywhere in a very short time."

"I'd vote for one of the streets near Virginia Wagner's house," Agatha said. "Any one except hers. Why waste time wandering through the woods when you could walk innocently down one of the streets that are nearest to Humboldt's cabin? Even if you're seen in the street, so what?"

"Why not Mrs. Wagner's street?" Giles asked.

"You'd risk being seen by her or being caught up with by her on the path if she was moving fast."

"You're assuming that the killer knew about Virginia Wagner's weekly visits," Giles said. "He probably didn't. Further, she said she took a roundabout path to avoid being seen. She and the killer were not necessarily using the same route."

"Sure, Mr. Sullivan, but wouldn't the killer use the same reasoning?"

"Then it's reasonable," Giles said, "to assume the killer entered the woods long before Mrs. Wagner did."

"Why would he do that?" Isabel asked. "The longer he hung around Humboldt's cabin, the greater the chance of being seen accidentally. If he got there at, say, nine o'clock, why didn't he knock on Humboldt's door then?"

"A good point," Giles said. "I think we can assume that he didn't get there early. If he had, and Humboldt let him in, it means they were talking for almost an hour. It's reasonable to assume that Humboldt took him into the study so Virginia Wagner could slip into the bedroom while Humboldt slipped the visitor out. Surely Humboldt could have gotten rid of his visitor before Mrs. Wagner came if he had come appreciably before nine-forty-five."

"This shows something else," Isabel said. "The visitor would not have been let in at all if he came early." At Giles's puzzled look, Isabel explained. "Why did the killer choose Saturday night just before ten? Because he was sure Humboldt would *not* let him in at any time. Either he knew about Virginia Wagner and Humboldt or he didn't. If he didn't, the odds against his choosing that particular day and time by accident are a hundred to one. No, in spite of their caution, the killer had to know about the weekly trysts."

"He must have been watching Humboldt's cabin for weeks," Agatha said, "to figure out the pattern, knowing that the door was unlocked for about fifteen minutes."

"Exactly." Isabel was glowing. "He knew that Humboldt unlocked the front door about nine-forty-five and that Virginia came between that time and ten. He knew that was the one time he could get in to see Humboldt at home secretly."

"He also didn't have much to say," Agatha said. "Since he was gone in—" She stopped. "Miss Macintosh, you've been to his house; did Humboldt have sliding bolts or dead bolts on his back door?"

"Both kinds on both doors."

"So the killer had to leave by the front door," Agatha said. "Otherwise he couldn't pin the murder on Virginia. This meant he had only about five minutes, at most, to do whatever he had in mind to do before Virginia came in. Any more time and she might have seen him leaving. He didn't know if she'd be a few minutes early or a few minutes late. If he came with the idea of killing Humboldt, the smart thing to do would be to walk into the house the moment Humboldt unlocked the door and stab him in the back. Then there'd be no danger of Virginia's seeing him come out of the cabin and no danger of his not finding the right sword on the wall—you once said Humboldt was always moving them around—and no danger of Humboldt grabbing another sword off the wall and dueling him."

"That's good, Agatha," Giles said. "So the killer came

to the house to have a very short discussion with Humboldt, such as 'Where have you buried the treasure?' after which, if he got a satisfactory answer, he would just leave."

"And if he got an unsatisfactory answer, he would just kill Humboldt?" Isabel asked. "Why not just go away anyway and give Humboldt a chance to think things over. You could always kill him next week."

"Maybe you couldn't," Agatha said. "Maybe Humboldt would change his routine once the killer got in this way; maybe he'd even stop seeing Virginia so the killer couldn't get into his house again."

"There are lots of places to kill Humboldt," Isabel said. "In the wood on the way to his office, for one. No, it was done this way because the killer had only one shot: either something irrevocable would happen the next week or—or something."

"Possibly," Oliver said, "the mere act of confrontation is the key. Once the killer is known to Professor Humboldt, he could protect himself against the killer, take reprisals, hide the treasure, do something that would prevent the killer from attaining his goal. There would be no second chance."

"I think you've got it, Oliver," Giles said. "The killer was someone who wanted something from Humboldt which, if Humboldt did not do, or give, would require that he be murdered."

"Or the opposite, sir. Possibly if Professor Humboldt were to refrain from doing something, he would not be killed."

"So our killer," Giles said, "is a person who knew Humboldt and whom Humboldt knew and did not fear. He was able to watch Humboldt's house every Saturday night for a period of weeks. He wanted Humboldt to do or to give him something, or to refrain from doing something, badly enough to kill for. The deal had to be simple enough to explain in a few minutes or else was one that had already been analyzed and required only acquiescence. He was in a position or condition where he could be hurt by Humboldt so badly that Humboldt had to be killed if they did not make the deal. Now, who do you know who fits the bill?"

"Leaving out the part about deals," Agatha said, "practically everybody on campus fits that description. Virginia Wagner, the six assistant professors, a dozen graduate students, all of Humboldt's students, half the professors, all the administrators, and Isabel Macintosh."

"Oh, come on, Agatha," Giles said, "you don't seriously think that— Why, Isabel was with me every minute of the time."

"She never went to the ladies' room, for one?"

"Well, of course. So she was out of my sight for a few minutes."

"Miss Macintosh." Agatha looked directly at Isabel. "How long would it take you to bike to the wood from Fathead's house?"

"A minute or less."

"How long to jog the quarter mile to Humboldt's cabin?"

"Two minutes, at most."

"How long to stab him?"

"Ten seconds, but you have to figure a little talking. I say, 'Fabian, darling, I've loved you for, lo, these many moons. Will you do me the honor of giving me your hand in marriage?' And he says, 'No. You're too skinny.' *Then* I kill him. Say one or two minutes."

"Fine. Total time, there and back, eight minutes. Was Miss Macintosh out of your sight, Mr. Sullivan, for a period of eight minutes?"

"Of course she was, several times. Just as I was out of her sight. But there's no connection between Isabel and the murder."

"An experienced writer for *The Daily Sleaze* could find a dozen connections," Agatha said warningly. "You've got till Wednesday, Mr. Sullivan. Don't mess up."

 **20**

"**I** NEVER THREATENED PROFESSOR HUMBOLDT," BRUCE Yablonski said, putting the baby on the floor. "Mrs. Wagner is lying."

Helen Yablonski, just plain tired, set the plastic tea tray on the coffee table and served Isabel and Giles. "Bruce wouldn't threaten anyone, Dean Macintosh," she said. "It's not our style."

"He threatened *you*, Bruce," Isabel said. "Didn't he?"

"It wasn't really a threat," Bruce said. "He was very interested in finding out who constructed the extra puzzles, that's all, and said, in effect, that he would take his marbles and go home if we didn't produce what he wanted. A very aggressive personality at work there, you understand, verging on paranoia."

"You didn't see this as a threat, Dr. Yablonski?"

"Well, of course it could have had some extremely negative long-term effects, had it been carried out."

"And now it won't?" Isabel probed. "So Professor Humboldt's death was beneficial to you?"

"Not really." Bruce's forehead grew moist. "There will be a—some difficulty during the transition period—I'll have to analyze the test results and curves—it will take time, and we may have to postpone publication...."

"You intend to take charge of the Project?"

"Well, Karen and I are the senior people—"

"Actually, Dr. Norstad has been here a year longer than you and Dr. Karas."

"He's just a statistician, a very narrow function. He doesn't have the overview."

"Wasn't Karen second in command? Without you?"

"It was just overseeing and collecting, basically. She's in English, so it wasn't appropriate— Humboldt always favored her. The psychological aspects were not given their proper weight; the Project wasn't *just* a technique for *English*; it should have been treated as an approach to *learning*."

"I was thinking of bringing in someone from the education department, a senior man, to lend authority to the Project," Isabel said.

"You can't do that." Bruce jumped up. "It's our Project; an outsider wouldn't know—"

"Can't I?" Isabel looked the plump young man in the eye. "Why not, Bruce? Six untenured assistant professors, hardly known outside these walls, practically unpublished—I wouldn't have the slightest difficulty."

Yablonski dropped his eyes. "K.K. and I—we could take over in a few weeks. We might even meet the publication date. It's a real innovation, lots of prestige for Windham."

"Hadn't you better concentrate on getting something of yours into print fast, Bruce?" Isabel said. "You're up for tenure this year, aren't you?"

He turned red. "You know, Miss Macintosh, Dean, the professor wouldn't let us publish anything about our work. It was all going to be in the book. I was going to have two papers in it with only his name and mine on them, two with Karen, and one with Carl. Isn't that enough?"

"Plenty, but they haven't been published yet."

"What are you getting at, Dean?" Bruce's wife had started to say something, but he placed his hand over hers. "You're acting as though you're waiting for me to do something."

"I was thinking, Bruce, just thinking, that I might serve on your tenure committee. And Karen's and Dag's too. With Professor Humboldt gone, the committee would welcome me. Of course, I'd have to spend a good deal of time looking into all the factors that would influence my decision."

Bruce glowered at Isabel. "You're beginning to sound more and more like Humboldt, Dean. What is your hidden agenda?"

"I want to find Humboldt's murderer, Bruce. Fast. And you're going to help me, aren't you, Assistant Professor Yablonski?"

Bruce looked at his wife. She reached out her hand to squeeze his, picked up the baby, and went into the kitchen. He licked his lips and said, "I get tenure and head the Project?"

"I'll look into your whole academic history as well as your work on the Project. If you've earned it, I'll recommend you for tenure. Just realize that my vote doesn't carry any more weight than anyone else's. On the other hand, some people do respect my judgment. As for heading the Project, you'll have to work that out with the others. If the Project is as good as I've heard, I'll not get in your way. Or Karen's either."

Bruce looked at her steadily. "What do you want, Dean?"

"I want to know who killed Professor Humboldt," Isabel said flatly.

"That's easy. The guy who constructed the seventh crossword. The three seventh crosswords."

Giles stepped in. "Do you know something we don't?"

"Facts, no, I don't think so. But I've been analyzing the facts we do know, as a psychologist, I mean. If the crosswords themselves were analyzed, the characteristics of the constructor would fit almost any professor at Windham. But the message of the crosswords themselves..."

"There was a message in the crosswords?" Giles asked.

"We found a set of words from the three puzzles that clearly showed Humboldt was a Nazi who had tortured people—Poles, actually—in concentration camps and was being hunted by killers for revenge. I—in the excitement of finding there was a message, even I joined in. But later I realized I could just as easily have put together a different message, one showing Humboldt was a saint, or anything in between."

"Given enough words to choose from," Giles said, "you can usually select a message to suit your needs. What made you think Humboldt was not a Nazi?"

"Oh, he was an anti-Semite all right—you should have heard some of the things he said to me. But if they wanted to kill him, why go to all the bother of constructing crosswords? Kidnap him—he lives in the wood, so that would be easy—torture him for a week, if that gives you pleasure, then kill him. Who needs crosswords?"

"True," Giles said. "A quick murder doesn't sound like a revenge killing. You've been to his house?"

"Of course. Three times. At the beginning of each year he has a gathering. One stiff hour, with dry sherry. But I found out something the first time that bears out my preliminary analysis of his personality. Humboldt was constipated."

"You looked into his medicine chest?" Isabel asked.

"Of course, just as I observed everything else about him. My professional life was in his hands."

"Let's get back to the key question," Giles said. "Who do you think constructed the seventh crosswords?"

"If there was no message *in* the crosswords, then the message *was* the crosswords."

"McLuhan?" Isabel said. "What was the message?"

"Precisely." Bruce beamed. "It said, 'I know all about the Project, I know the format you use, I know the box you use, I know when you meet, who does what, and how. I can disrupt the Project if I wish, so pay attention."

"If we accept that," Giles said, "why did the sender

use this means of sending the message, and what did he want?"

"It's—it was *very* hard to get a message to Professor Humboldt directly and *privately*, impossible if you didn't want it to be known who *you* were. Humboldt was crazy about puzzles. Good too. The best way to catch his attention was to give him a hard puzzle. As to what was wanted, I'm sure that would have been the next step. Or was."

Giles thought for a moment. "You're saying this tells us more about the killer."

"Obviously. He's someone known to Humboldt, both his appearance and voice. Further, the threat and, assuredly, the demand for whatever the killer wanted were involved with the Project, not only with Humboldt."

"Ah, yes," Giles said, "otherwise a rock through the window of Humboldt's house would have caught Humboldt's attention quite effectively, with much less effort and risk."

"It's conjectural and there may be some other explanation that fits the facts better," Bruce said overmodestly, "but I don't see it as of now."

"So the killer negotiated with Humboldt on Saturday night," Giles said, "and when Humboldt refused, killed him."

"Exactly. Therefore, the killer is one of those five. In the Project, I mean."

"Not six?" Isabel asked dryly.

"I know I didn't do it," Bruce said coolly.

"I don't," Isabel replied. "And there are lots of holes in your reasoning. First, just because you couldn't find a message in the puzzles doesn't mean there isn't any. I have some skill in this line, and Mr. Sullivan is an acknowledged expert. We will examine the puzzles this evening and see what we can find."

"The six of us," Bruce said, "are also experts. We were quite competent when Humboldt first selected us, and we've had three years of intensive practice since. I assure you, if we didn't find a message, it isn't there."

"Second," Isabel continued, "there is no certainty that the message, threat, or whatever, involves the Project merely because crossword puzzles were the vehicle for getting the information to Professor Humboldt. Third, there was no time for negotiation with Humboldt prior to his death. Even if there was, what could he have given the killer? Can you visualize the killer demanding a million dollars in small bills and getting angry because Humboldt had only large bills in the house?"

"It could have been something less physical," Bruce pointed out.

"What?" Isabel challenged. "A promise to leave all his money to the killer? To vote Democrat? To give the killer an A in his course? Is there anything intangible that couldn't be repudiated the next day? And reprisals taken against the demander afterward?"

"Something signed?" Bruce tried. "A contract to buy something, or sell, or to pay someone?"

"Unwitnessed?" Isabel was scornful. "To be negotiated in a few minutes? Or prepared in advance, thrust under Humboldt's nose, with a pen and orders to sign, unread? Worthless and unenforceable. And again, if the killer was so anxious not to be known to Humboldt, was vulnerable to Humboldt's actions regardless of what was signed, reprisals still could be taken."

"Then what do you think happened? Do you have anything that fits the facts better? Dean Macintosh?"

"Not yet," Isabel said, "but I will. Your reasoning may be full of holes, as of now at least, but I believe your conclusions are accurate. I'm going to start looking over the Project papers shortly, and maybe involve myself more deeply."

"You're trying to take over the Project." Bruce's face got red. "You have no right."

"Who does? You?" Isabel mocked. "All six of you? Humboldt's heirs, if any? Windham University? The State of Vermont?" Bruce sat silent, sullen. "The Project needs a senior professor as leader. I was a respected professor of literature here at Windham while you were still sweating out your Ph.D. You should be happy I'm even *considering* looking into the *possibility* of taking over—it's a lot of work I don't need right now for very little reward—instead of letting the Project die a natural death. You think the endowment for the Chair of Military History will fund the Project? Forget it. When he was alive, Humboldt could funnel a little of the money anywhere he saw fit and get away with it. Now? I could close the valve tomorrow; without the money you'd be out of business in one week. Unless you have a rich aunt you could kill? Fast?"

Giles spoke quickly. "I have a few more questions, Dr. Yablonski, if you don't mind. Where were you Saturday night between nine and eleven?"

"Do you think I did it?" Bruce looked ready to explode. "I just gave you my analysis, which shows someone in the Project did it. Doesn't that prove anything to you?"

"Yes, that you're an intelligent young man, which we both know. Please answer the question."

"I was home. Here. Ask my wife."

"You didn't leave the house at all?"

"Of course I did, a little before ten. But only for fifteen minutes. To go to the store."

"You ride a bicycle?"

"Everyone here does. Assistant professors can't afford cars."

"Do you also jog?"

"A little. When you lead a sedentary life, it's healthy."

"If you had to choose which of the other five killed Professor Humboldt, who would it be?"

"How was he killed?"

"The police are keeping it to themselves for now. Choose on the basis of personality."

"You have to take other things into account. If Humboldt was strangled, Carl Richter, definitely. He's big enough and has a very short fuse. With a knife? Jennifer Zapata. Poison? Pick Evelyn Tinguely. She just looks sweet and innocent; she's used to getting anything she wants from men, but to Humboldt she was just another pawn. Karen? She'd break every bone in his body with a club;

she's strong enough. If it was a timetable type of murder, where the killer was miles away when it happened, arrest Dag right now. Every one of them is a potential killer. Take your choice."

"My choice," Isabel said, getting up to go, "based solely on personality, motive, means, and opportunity, and, of course, intelligence, would be Dr. Bruce Yablonski."

◈◈◈◈◈◈◈◈◈◈◈◈◈◈◈◈◈◈◈ 21 ◈◈◈

"**A**RE WE GOING TO WALK TO PROFESSOR KARAS'S house?" Giles asked.

"To all of them," Isabel said. "Rockfield isn't all that big, and the staff has a tendency to cluster near the campus."

"Do you really think Yablonski did it?"

"I really think he *could* have done it. Do you think a sweet-looking young Jewish intellectual *couldn't*?"

"No, no, I know that anyone could commit murder. What I meant was, is he really your first choice, Isabel, or were you just trying to stir things up?"

"Both. Bruce has a genius IQ; we all have great hopes for him. He's smart enough to figure out how to kill Humboldt and get away with it. And he has—did you see how he was holding the baby? And the way he looked at his wife? Wouldn't you have killed for your wife, Giles?"

"I would have, Isabel, and I would kill for you too. But that doesn't mean I would commit murder, coldblooded murder."

"You don't know what you'd do, Giles, until the moment arrived. Remember the Brundage case? Wait until you meet the others, the other five from the Project. Every one of them is a nice person, intelligent, competent, productive—even Zapata—the kind of kid you'd be proud to have for a son. Or daughter."

"Do you think one of them did it?"

"I wasn't sure before; now I am."

"Because of what Bruce said?"

"If he thinks one of them did it, Giles, so do I. I can't see any other possibility right now."

"What about that Nazi business?"

"Highly improbable. I didn't particularly like Humboldt, but I think I would have sensed if he were a Nazi."

Giles walked silently for a minute. "Has anything unusual happened with the Project recently? Other than the three extra crosswords?"

"Not that I've noticed, but I haven't been observing the Project particularly closely. I'll ask Karen Karas."

"Why don't you let me handle this, Isabel? Oliver and I—"

"This is my place," she said fiercely, "not yours. It's my university and my professor who was murdered. It's probably one of my professors who killed him. You want me to turn aside? To say 'it's not my table'? Is that really what you expect of me, Giles?"

"No, Isabel," Giles said tenderly. "You know what I think of you. It's just—I'm beginning to get worried about you, Isabel. First, Yablonski says you're beginning to sound more and more like Humboldt. Then you're going to take Humboldt's place on the tenure committees. Now you're going to be the lead professor on the Project." Giles took a few more steps, then spoke again. "Tell me, Isabel, would an assistant professor kill for tenure?"

 **22** ❖❖❖

IT WAS THE FIRST TIME ISABEL HAD SEEN KAREN KARAS
in a dress, and she was pleasantly surprised at how much
more feminine Karen looked in the dress than in the pant-
suits she usually wore in school. "I've been looking forward to your lecture, Mr. Sullivan," Karen said. "I was
going to ask you, if you could spare the time, to criticize
the Project's puzzles, just a random sampling. I'm concerned that we've become inbred."

"I'd be happy to," Giles said, and as he caught Isabel's
look added, "next Sunday, after the lecture. My week is
quite organized."

"We'd be grateful for whatever time you could spare,"
Karen said graciously.

"Is your husband home?" Isabel asked. "Somehow I've
not yet had the pleasure of meeting him."

"He's very busy," Karen said, "and hardly gets out.
Poetry is very hard work. I know; I've tried it." She
walked to the door in the rear of the apartment, knocked,
and stuck her head in. There was a moment's whispered

112

discussion, then they both came into the living room. "Dean Macintosh, this is my husband, Chris. Chris, this is Dean Isabel Macintosh—you've heard me speak of her—and Mr. Giles Sullivan, the eminent attorney and crossword expert who was—is—going to lecture next Sunday."

"How do you do, Dean, Mr. Sullivan," Chris Karas said in a low, sweet voice. He was three inches shorter than his wife and at least ten years older. Balding, with a small thickening around his waist, he wasn't Isabel's idea of a Romeo, but Karen's eyes softened when she looked at him. After a bit of small talk he excused himself to go back to his room; he was working on his epic poem, he explained, and was far behind schedule. It was to be entered in a contest for unpublished poets, Karen told them. It was very hard for a poet to become known, and unless you were published, there was no hope of even a non-tenure-track instructorship.

"I once read," Isabel said, "that the most important attribute of a professional poet was a working wife. Your husband, Dr. Karas, is doubly blessed in having a wife so well thought of in her field."

"I'm so pleased to hear that from you," Karen said. "I read some of your papers when I was a graduate student here and I was very impressed. It was a great loss to the department when you went into administration." Karen hesitated for a moment, then said, "I know it's poor form, Dean, but this is very important to me. You said I was well thought of in my field. Does this carry over into the English department?"

"You're concerned about your tenure," Isabel said, "naturally. The problem is, as you know, publication."

"I have—we all have—written several papers, good papers, based on the work we're doing for the Project. Professor Humboldt wanted them all to appear at the same time, for impact, in the book he was preparing. He felt the techniques we originated, and which evolved into the standardized system we are now using routinely, would have a greater chance of rapid acceptance, of being put into practice, if all the data and the remarkable results we've achieved were presented as a unified whole."

"The fact remains, Dr. Karas, that none of you has published a word for three years. I don't know if your tenure committee will accept unpublished work on the Project as evidence of scholarship."

"But we *can* publish. Our work is practically done. Professor Humboldt assured us that the book would appear this fall."

"Professor Humboldt isn't around anymore, Karen."

"I was his deputy, Dean. I can take over. I'll work night and day, do anything. I know almost everything Professor Humboldt was planning."

Isabel looked into Karen's pleading eyes. "Scholarly books make very little money, Karen. Your share couldn't possibly be enough to pay for a vanity-press publication of your husband's epic."

Karen flushed. "I guess it isn't very hard to read my mind, but why not? Every man deserves a chance, one chance at least. If I were sure of getting tenure, I could take out a loan."

"No one can be sure, Karen, but if it will make you feel any better, I told Bruce I would look into serving on the three tenure committees; Dag's too. But," Isabel said, "all I can do is to make sure your scholarship is evaluated properly."

"But all we have to show is the Project," Karen said.

"I am also considering adding my name to the Project," Isabel said. "If all six of you agree. There is no way the book will see print without at least one senior professor's cooperation. I don't know anyone else in the university who is qualified and who is sufficiently knowledgeable about crosswords who would allow his name to be used without studying your work for at least a year."

"Another year would ruin us all. I would be honored if you would let us use your name. Our deal was that Professor Humboldt got half the money. It isn't much, but it's all we can offer you. At least the endowment paid for some of the expenses."

"Tell me about the Liberman Prize, Karen."

"How did you hear about that? It was supposed to be a secret. Did you tell anyone else?"

"I have my sources, and I haven't told anyone, Karen, so don't get upset. Everyone in education and reading knows about it; how did you and Professor Humboldt think you could keep your involvement a secret?"

"That we were going to submit the Project for the Prize was the secret. Everybody we know of is working along traditional lines, trying to improve rather than innovate. We have a truly scientific approach, rigorous methodology, and standardized puzzles. Our fear was that one of the huge schools would take our techniques, dump in tons of money and hundreds of people, maybe get foundation backing, and take over a school district in a minority neighborhood in a big city, such as New York. The publicity they would get would wipe us off the map. Worse, they might even fail, for a variety of reasons, including haste. If that happened, the whole idea would be discredited forever. Everybody, especially the kids, would lose. Everybody."

"Including you?"

"Including all of us. We've put three years of our lives, our professional careers, into the Project. No one is going to stop us. No one."

"Bruce thinks you and he can run it all by yourselves. And I'm not too sure he wants you around."

"Bruce is overreaching, as usual. We need all the help we can get. If half the money isn't enough, Dean, I'm sure we'd all agree to take less for ourselves."

"I'm not interested in the money, Karen. The only doubt I have is if I can handle the job. If it weren't that I have to look into the Project so deeply anyway, I wouldn't have considered the involvement."

Karen lifted her eyebrows. "You're investigating the murder?"

"Actually," Isabel said, "Mr. Sullivan is; I'm just tagging along. Bruce is certain the murderer is the constructor of the seventh puzzles."

Karen thought for a moment. "He may be right, although there is no direct evidence of any kind. The extra puzzles are the only unusual things that have happened to Professor Humboldt recently. That I'm aware of, at least."

"Dr. Yablonski also thinks"—Giles entered the conversation—"that the constructor of the puzzles is one of you six."

"That's also probable, Mr. Sullivan. But again, we have no direct evidence."

"Where were you between nine and eleven Saturday night, Professor Karas?"

Karen colored, but answered in an even tone. "Here. At home. We rarely go out."

"Your husband will attest to this? Is he the only— Was anyone else with you?"

"We were alone; he is the only witness to my alibi. But I must tell you, he wouldn't be a very good witness."

"Because he'd lie for you?"

"Of course he would—he's my husband—and anything else that would be needed to protect me. That includes killing for me, if necessary; poets are not always soft creatures. But that isn't what I meant. Chris was in his room all night; he wouldn't know where I was."

"Did you stay in the house all night?" Giles asked.

"No. I went out for about an hour. Jogging. Between nine and ten, unfortunately."

"Did you see anyone, Dr. Karas?"

"You mean did anyone see me? Yes, a few other joggers. We waved. But I'm not sure they knew who I was; I couldn't tell who they were. It was a dark night."

"How were you dressed?"

"Jogging clothes. Running shoes. Sweatband. Fluorescent straps aren't necessary around here if you stay on the side streets."

"Did you see anyone wearing a dark raincoat and a hat? Not necessarily jogging; walking, perhaps."

"No. Why? Did he see me?"

"Did you jog in Windham Wood?"

"Certainly not; you could twist your ankle, even with a light."

"Do you know where Professor Humboldt's house is? How to get there?"

"Of course. I've been there several times. I know where everyone's house is in the wood; Chris and I love to hike there."

"What was your relationship with Professor Humboldt?"

"It used to be very good, but lately I felt he was picking on me. He had been very nasty to all of us in the past few months, but for the past week he was acting as though I were to blame for whatever was bothering him."

"He blamed you for the additional puzzles?"

"Not directly, but he acted as though I had failed him, that if I just had the courage, the good sense, to apply the red-hot pincers in the right places, I'd have had a confession the first day."

"Who do you think constructed the puzzles, Professor?"

"How should I know? What did Bruce say? He was to have the psychological profiles ready today."

"Suppose I were to tell you you were his first choice."

"Good old Bruce. I don't think he does it consciously, and he'd deny it if you showed him the evidence, but he's very jealous. He's sure he should have headed the Project in my place."

"Do you head the Project? I thought Professor Humboldt did."

"He does. Did. I'm sort of second in command."

"One more thing, Professor Karas. Bruce said the message you found in the crosswords, the one about Professor Humboldt being a Nazi, was not true. How do you feel?"

Karen answered slowly and thoughtfully. "It would not be completely inconsistent with what I consider him capable of, but it is so unlikely that I would place no reliance on it. If there is a message in the puzzles, that isn't it."

"Yet you all agreed, at the time, that was the message."

"We were searching desperately for an answer. At the time it seemed reasonable. On reflection I no longer think so."

117

"Who do you think is the most likely constructor of the puzzles, Dr. Karas?"

"Would it sound like tit for tat if I said Bruce? I don't care; he's my choice."

"Bruce says the puzzles themselves are the message."

"It seems to me, Mr. Sullivan"—Karen smiled sadly—"that the murder is the message."

 **23** ✦✦

"**A**RE THEY ALL LIKE THAT?" GILES ASKED.

"Like what?" Isabel asked.

"Nice, sweet, intelligent, helpful young men and women," Giles replied. "People with normal human worries and troubles, loyal to their families, trying to get ahead."

"Do you still subscribe, subconsciously, to Lombroso's theories?" Isabel was shocked. "That you can tell criminals by their physical characteristics?"

"No. Not really. I don't think I do. It's just that— If they're all like the two we've just seen— Can you imagine either of them killing Professor Humboldt? Sticking a knife into his heart?"

"Good point, Sullivan. When we come to the one with the horns and the tail, we'll know who the killer is. Simple."

"That's not what I meant, Isabel, and you know it. What I meant was—"

"I know, darling, and I understand. What you meant was that it would pain you to find that Karen Karas was the killer and you'd have to turn her over to the police and her husband would never get his poems published. Or to take Bruce Yablonski away from his family and leave that sweet-looking young wife to take care of four children without a father."

"Sort of like that. Well, yes, I do. Mean that, I mean. Don't you feel the same?"

"More than you, Giles. So what do you want to do? Give up? Leave it to the police? You know they'll never solve a case like this; it's not the sort of thing they're used to."

"I don't want to give up, Isabel; a murderer must be punished. Or, at least, tried by a jury of his peers. It's just that there will be no—no pleasure in solving this case."

"I learned, long ago, Giles, that not everything you do brings you pleasure. Or even satisfaction. There are things we must do because they're right."

"When someone tells me that, I know it's going to hurt."

"There's no middle way, Giles. If you don't solve it, it won't be solved. You either do or you don't. But cheer up, darling. You may be in luck. From the way things are shaping up, you won't be able to solve this case."

 **24** ❖❖❖

"**I**F YOU THINK THE OTHER TWO LOOKED LIKE CHOIR-boys," Isabel said, "wait till you meet this one. He's not only a mathematician; he's a statistician, the dullest discipline in the school. And he's Norwegian, one of those cold, quiet types that won't walk on the grass."

There was no response, so Isabel knocked again. "We're a few minutes early, according to Aggie's schedule. If he isn't home, we'll—"

The door opened. Dag Norstad was wearing a port-colored velvet dressing gown and clearly nothing else, not even slippers. "You are too early," he said. "Can you come back in fifteen minutes?"

"We're on a tight schedule, Dr. Norstad." Isabel pushed her way into the apartment. What was obviously the bedroom door was closing as they entered. Isabel caught a flash of long black hair and pink skin. Dag ungraciously led them to the living room chairs. The Sunday papers were scattered on the floor. Dag made no attempt to pick them up.

"We'll make it quick," Isabel said. "Don't bother bringing out the tea. Or the crumpet."

Dag looked puzzled. "If you would like some tea—"

"Or the English muffin," Isabel said. "Forget it; just an old American saying. We came—this is Mr. Giles Sullivan, the great detective—we came to talk to you about the Humboldt murder."

"Yes. Miss Parrot told me I would be discussing this with you at three P.M. sharp."

"Yes, well, sorry about the scheduling error."

"Mistake," Dag corrected her. "An error is something incorrect that is inherent in the measuring process; it can be compensated for, often, and its range is numerable. Always you can be aware of an error. A mistake is not predictable, cannot be adjusted for, and is often difficult to find. Mistakes, however, are avoidable; errors are not."

"Then I'm sorry for the mistake of coming too early, Dr. Norstad," Isabel said. "And now that my English mistake has been corrected, let's continue. Tell me about the seventh puzzle."

"There were seventh puzzles inserted into the Project assignments three times, Dr. Macintosh. The probability of this being a mistake or an accident is very low."

"And your conclusion, Dr. Norstad?"

"The purpose of the puzzles was to communicate something to Professor Humboldt, something which would injure the Project. Professor Humboldt's actions were a confirmation."

"Why should anyone want to harm the Project?"

"It is by no means certain that the Project was to be damaged. Possibly it was to obtain something of value from Professor Humboldt."

"What did the professor have that anyone could want? I didn't know he was rich."

"I do not know that either," Dag said. "But it is not always what one has that is valuable, but what one can control, what one can do."

"Tenure? Recognition? Recommendation? What is within the power of a university professor to give?"

"All of these, certainly. But also, is it not valuable to

withhold? For example, if I know that Carl's degree was obtained in an incorrect way, is it not good for Carl that I do not tell the dean of faculty? Or that Bruce is making a graduate assistant pregnant and I do not tell his wife?"

"Are those facts, Dag?"

"Examples. I have been thinking. If Professor Humboldt is not rich in something I want but has something I do not want him to give to other people, that is enough reason to warn him. Do not hurt me and I do not hurt you."

"Yet he was hurt, Dag. Permanently."

"If I had the fear the professor could tell about me, is it not better I fix it so he can not tell ever?"

"Bruce says that the killer is the one who constructed the seventh puzzles."

"I have insufficient information to decide, but there is no other person it could be, I think."

"And he is one of you six?"

"Again, it is only a belief, but I agree."

"Which one, Dr. Norstad?"

"Zapata is the most reasonable. Professor Humboldt told her, many times, her qualifications were not good."

"That's not what you said before. About his knowing something the killer didn't want known."

"Professor Humboldt was a very careful researcher. Before he accused, he would have data. Perhaps Zapata performed plagiarism on her thesis, or used a threat to receive her position. She was all the time making threats."

"Or sex?" Isabel suggested. Dag shook his head. "Different people have different tastes, Dr. Norstad."

"Not Zapata. Tinguely, of course, is possible; even Karas. But Zapata?" He smiled the smile of a connoisseur instructing an amateur.

"Where were you," Giles asked, "between nine and eleven last night?"

"You are an official from the government, sir?" Dag asked. "You have the right to ask this?"

"I'm giving him the right," Isabel said. "As dean of faculty I have a great interest in who is granted tenure. I will also become deeply involved in the Project shortly.

If you do not want to cooperate with us, say so, and we will leave at once."

Dag weighed Isabel for a moment, then answered. "I was at the Student Union."

"Did anyone see you there?" Giles asked.

"Of course. Many."

"Were you with anyone in particular?"

"Not at first, Mr. Sullivan."

"You picked up a lady?"

"I like to make friends," Dag said. "New friends."

Giles turned to Isabel. "How far from Professor Humboldt's house to the Student Union?"

"Same as from President Jordan's house," she said. "Like the two legs of a triangle."

"Do you jog, Dr. Norstad?" Giles asked.

"I run. Much more healthy."

"Do you know how to get to Professor Humboldt's house?"

"Of course. I have been there three times."

"Could you have slipped away from the Student Union and run to Professor Humboldt's house last night?"

"Any one of a hundred people could have done that, and no one would know who was away for that time. But I would not run in the forest at night; to walk would take very little more time."

"Did you do that? Go to his house?"

"I went outside once, for fresh air; that is all."

"So you have no alibi, Dr. Norstad?"

Dag shrugged his shoulders apologetically. "Who has an alibi for that time, of him I would be most suspicious."

"What motive would you have for killing Professor Humboldt?"

"The exact same as the others. I would also be the most suspicious of the person who did not have a motive. Would you not?"

"I would," Isabel said as they left. "But that doesn't mean the person with a motive is innocent."

 **25**

"**S**O MUCH FOR SHY, WITHDRAWN STATISTICIANS," GILES said outside. "After my glimpse of the secret world of the puritanical Virginia Wagner, and aware of what evil lurks in the heart of the overtly decorous dean of faculty, can I expect that the straitlaced Vermont-schoolmarm type, Agatha Parrot, is really Master of the Revels at the local Hell-Fire Club and that our alluring sociologist, Evelyn Tinguely, is, to the frustration of the local rakes, a dedicated virgin?"

"After five years as dean," Isabel said, walking faster, "I thought nothing would surprise me anymore, but this case, it's like turning over a rock."

"There's nothing really wrong with a single young man entertaining a young lady in his quarters."

"There really is"—Isabel was thinking of the two girls who cried for an hour in her office the past Monday—"if she's a student of his, and particularly if she's a freshman."

"Neither of which you know. Do you disapprove of sexual relations between the sexes?"

"A teacher is *in loco parentis*. It's like incest. Worse. There may be a tendency to compromise standards. It's very hard to flunk a girl who's just jumped out of your bed; the grade you give her may reflect skills in areas completely outside her major."

"It's also sex discrimination against boys," Giles joked.

"Not necessarily," Isabel muttered, reminded of other problems she had faced in the past.

"You're not hinting that Professor Humboldt...?"

"I'm not sure of anything anymore, Giles. I used to look at the world, when I was younger, with certainty. I knew who I was, I knew where I stood. Now the earth is moving under my feet."

"This case...?"

"When I found out about the seventh puzzles, I had it all figured out. We would question them all and after that, after we had gotten all the information, after we sized up each one of them, we'd concentrate the pressure on the right one, two at the most, and that would be it. Now...?"

"Now Dag Norstad is on your list of possibles too?"

"He was never off it, just near the bottom, slightly above Evelyn Tinguely."

"All because he had a girl in his apartment on a Sunday afternoon in spring?"

"No, because *I* misjudged him. I don't have a list anymore; they're all Number One."

"Who was at the top of your list?"

"Carl Richter. You'll meet him soon. He's still the first among equals, I guess. A big physical type. In another environment he could easily be a killer of some kind."

"There are all kinds of people, Isabel, who could kill. Police, doctors, soldiers, judges—I'm grateful they're around to protect me. And to save me from doing my own killing."

"And these people have characteristics that differentiate them from most other people in some way."

"You were wrong about Oliver, weren't you, Isabel?"

"That's different. He was—he's in disguise. And he

would not kill in anger, would he? Or out of fear?"

"Oliver? No, he's a professional. So you think Carl Richter has the look of a killer? Lombroso comes home to roost?"

"Judge for yourself when you see him. And judge again when you meet Evelyn."

"Who's second on your list of killers?"

"Bruce. Yes, Bruce Yablonski. There are fat killers, you know. Not that he's a typical killer, but he—he analyzes logically. If he thought that Humboldt had to die to save himself or his family, he'd figure out very quickly— he's a genius, you know—how to do it, how to get away with it, and then he'd act. With no hesitation."

"I tend to agree. Who's third? Zapata?"

"I'm not sure; it's a toss-up between her and Karas."

"I don't see Karen—"

"Because she's sweet and soft-looking? Lovable? You don't see the claws of the mother cat either, but just try hurting one of her kittens."

"But isn't Zapata the revolutionary, the one who's always threatening to blow up North America?"

"She spends an awful lot of time talking about it with her Marxist buddies, but she's never done anything violent that I know of. And she puts in a lot of time with the poor kids, the adults, too, in Rockfield. They all love her. Maybe all that talk is cathartic."

Giles stopped walking. "Why are we knocking ourselves out like this, interviewing six people in one day? What have we learned so far? What do you expect to learn from this? These are all very bright people. Do you really think that if one of them is the killer, he will accidentally say something that points to himself?"

"Maybe. Intelligence has nothing to do with it. If the killer reveals a clue to his identity, it will not be because of stupidity; it will be because he, as the killer, had to answer a certain question in a certain way. For all we know, we may have already been given the vital clue."

"If we have," Giles grumbled, "I'm not aware of it."

"We'll discuss it tonight, all of us."

"Oliver too? And Miss Parrot?"

"Four heads are better than two."

"But I thought— Weren't we . . . ?"

"I'm not in the mood."

They walked on in silence. Isabel took Giles's hand. "But if we come up with a good lead . . ."

 **26**

THE SOUND OF A HARPSICHORD TWINKLED THROUGH the doorway around Carl Richter's broad shoulders. "Scarlatti?" Isabel asked.

"It's relaxing," Carl said, taking his finger out of the book and slipping the library card in to mark his place.

"Is that a math book?" Isabel asked.

"On *teaching* math," Carl said. "All week long, between the Project and my classes, I work on reading. Occasionally I have to remind myself that there are other things to learn and to teach. To teach how to teach."

"This is Giles Sullivan," Isabel said, "my friend and—"

"I know. Bruce phoned me—everybody, I guess—and warned me what to expect. A thorough grilling, complete with carrot and sticks. I'm Carl Richter, Number Two Suspect according to Bruce." He thrust his huge hand out to Giles.

Giles took the hand cautiously, but, like so many big men, Carl shook hands gently. "Exactly what did Bruce tell you, Mr. Richter?" Giles asked.

129

"That Dean Macintosh is acting in an uncharacteristic manner, using open threats and bribes instead of her usual subtle hints, her iron-fist-in-the-velvet-glove technique. Call me Carl, Mr. Sullivan." He turned to Isabel. "You must be very upset to be acting this way."

"What do you think," she snapped. "One of my professors is murdered by another. I lose two good teachers, the publicity will be horrible, and God knows what dirt the reporters will turn up."

"Are you sure," Carl asked, "that one of us did it?"

"Aren't you? You think it was pure coincidence that he was killed the day after the seventh crossword appeared, the third one?"

"What evidence do you have, Dean, that it wasn't coincidental? And even if there was a connection, does it necessarily follow that whoever constructed the puzzle killed Professor Humboldt? And even if that was the case, was it necessarily one of us? The Project group, I mean? Or anyone connected with the school for that matter? Setting hypothesis on top of conjecture resting on assumption may be acceptable in literary games, but for a rigorous analysis you must start from a firm foundation."

"I have no proof yet, Dr. Richter, but neither is this a mathematical exercise where every step has to be demonstrably valid before the next step can be taken. In real-life problems you work on probability, not certainty, and everything we've found out so far bears out my original impression: that one of you killed Professor Humboldt, and that the seventh crossword is deeply implicated, central to the crime."

"Oh, I agree with that," Carl said easily. "I just want you to keep your options open in case some townie decides to confess." He started to say something, stopped, then took the bull by the horns. "No offense intended, Dean, but who elected you detective?"

"Lou Quesada is a good security chief, not a detective. The police are no better for crimes of this type. We've gotten further in one day, less than a day, than they could in a week. And Mr. Sullivan solved an even more mysterious crime just a few months ago in New York."

"One crime doth not a Sherlock make."

"If you think you can do better, Richter, have at it. Meanwhile, you're a prime suspect, so we want you to answer some questions."

"And if I refuse?"

"I hope that's a rhetorical question, Richter, because if I thought you meant it—"

"Just teasing, Dean. I didn't realize how uptight you were. And yes, I really love Windham and would love to be granted tenure. So, I do jog, I do know where Humboldt's cabin is, although I don't think I could find it in the dark, and between nine and eleven I was in the weight room of the gym—I have a key—working out. No one else was there."

"Did Bruce tell you everything?"

"Twice. You really shook him up, Dean."

"Isn't it unusual," Giles asked, "for a young man, a single young man, to spend Saturday night in the gym?"

"I don't drink, Mr. Sullivan, and I don't enjoy the bar scene or one-night stands. My girl—we broke up two weeks ago and I'm not in the mood to meet anyone else. If it happens, it happens, but that's all."

"I'm sure you'll—" Giles realized how fatuous it would sound. "I hear you hated Humboldt, Richter. Carl."

"Sort of. Not really hate. But how are you supposed to feel if the guy who holds your future in his hands threatens to destroy it. Your future, I mean. Was I supposed to love him?"

"Did you hate him enough to kill him, Carl?"

"Sometimes. But when I cooled off, the feeling went away. And think about this, Mr. Sullivan. How was he supposed to tell the other members of my tenure committee what a great scholar I was, in spite of my not having published in three years, if he was dead? If you'll tell me how I gained anything by killing him, we can discuss this matter further. I'm really not the type to kill for pleasure, or to risk jail either."

"You may have a motive we don't know about, Carl. Did you have any relationship, contact even, with Professor Humboldt, other than through the Project?"

"We're both members of the Crossword Club—all of us are—and I attended his lectures when I was first appointed. That's all."

"You're sure? You realize, if we find out that you had any other contact at all, no matter how innocent, and you deny it now, it points the finger of suspicion directly at you."

"Don't belabor the obvious, Mr. Sullivan; I'm not a fool."

"Do you know, or have you heard, anything about any of your six colleagues who had anything at all to do with Professor Humboldt, no matter how minor, outside the Project?"

"No, but I'm not the one to know. Mrs. Wagner. She knew everything he did. Ask her."

"Who do you think constructed the seventh puzzle?"

"If it was one of us, Bruce, probably. His mind works that way."

"Why would Bruce do it?"

"To annoy Humboldt? Because Bruce thought it was funny? To see how Humboldt would react?"

"But Humboldt's reaction could have seriously damaged Bruce's chances of tenure, along with yours and the others. Bruce is a psychologist; wouldn't he have known how Humboldt would react?"

"Bruce isn't as smart as he thinks he is. Obviously he didn't think Humboldt would react the way he did."

"Then you think Bruce killed Humboldt?"

Carl thought for a while, then said, "No. I just don't see that. It isn't in his makeup."

"In whose makeup is it, Carl? Besides yours, I mean. Dag's? Karen's? Jennifer's? Evelyn's?"

Carl's face got red and his jaw muscles tightened. He walked over to the apartment entrance door, yanked it open, and jerkily motioned Giles and Isabel to get out.

 **27**

"CARL RICHTER ISN'T QUITE AS CONTROLLED AS HE would like others to think," Giles said.

"No one is," Isabel said. "But you were deliberately baiting him; I could tell. I'd hate to be on the stand with you cross-examining me."

"I just wanted to see how he'd react," Giles said.

"You saw, all right. You were lucky I was there to protect you."

"As long as I have my cane—"

"He would have torn you apart before you could untwist the cane, Giles. He's half your age. And what kind of reaction did you expect? The poor guy lost his girl—he's obviously a one-girl-at-a-time guy—and he lost the guy who was going to make him famous overnight and get him tenure. Can you imagine what it means to an education professor to be associated with the Project? If it really works that well?"

"They're all in that position, Isabel. Whichever one of them killed Humboldt must have had something much more important than fame and tenure to gain. Or lose."

"To an assistant professor there's nothing more important," Isabel said. "Let's stop in here for a while, Sullivan; my throat is dry, and I don't want to face Jennifer Zapata with a vitamin-deficiency disease."

"This is not New York, Macintosh. Can you—For thou on honey-dew hath fed, and drunk the milk of Paradise—can you possibly stomach ersatz?"

"Have no fear, Sullivan, I've taught them how to make a real egg cream."

 **28**

JENNIFER ZAPATA, WEARING BIG GLASSES ON HER THIN, dark little face, was sitting at a table covered with ledgers and neat piles of papers when Isabel and Giles responded to her yelled, "Come in."

"That doesn't look at all like third world studies," Isabel remarked as Jennifer motioned her and Giles to draw chairs up to the table, "or the Project."

"Bookkeeping," Jennifer said. "Those stupid morons in the food co-op think that all they have to do is get start-up funding and everything goes by itself. They don't even have inventory control."

"And you do it for them?"

"One more month, that's all. I told them. One more month and they're on their own. I mean it."

"Where did you learn bookkeeping?"

"I always knew it. Since I was ten I did it for my grandfather's store. It's just a way of balancing, so you know where everything is."

"Did you do it for your father too?"

"He doesn't need me; he's got hotshot accountants to show him how to screw the government."

"How does that background translate into third world studies?"

"Somebody's got to show them; they're too stupid to think one day ahead. As long as they've got their beans and TV—bread and circuses—they're coopted by every lying— You expect me to sit by a fountain in mantilla holding a white fan? Dolores del Rio? And wait for some rich moron to— Did you?"

"I didn't have the choice, Jennifer, then. Your parents?"

"My mother was worse than my father. When I was sixteen— Why do you want to hear this? You never took an interest in me before. As a woman."

"It's my way, Jennifer, of trying to get to know you while I'm trying to solve the Humboldt case. If I succeed, we'll all benefit; all except one, maybe. Finish the sentence, then we'll talk about the murder."

Jennifer looked at Isabel suspiciously, then said, "When I was sixteen—a priest, an endocrinologist, and a psychiatrist. The priest and the shrink knew *exactly* what was wrong with me; trouble was, they couldn't agree with each other. My mother still keeps sending me news about the nice young men, her friends' sons, and friends of friends. My father keeps writing that anytime I want to give up this childish foolishness—he still can't believe I'm over thirty—there's a job waiting for me as a vice-president—can you imagine the *sacrifice*, a female officer?—in his company, where I can put all my energy to work constructively. Okay? What about Humboldt?"

"One of you six killed him, Jennifer."

"Everybody knows that; what took you so long?"

"Was it you?"

"That's a stupid question. Would I tell you if I did?"

"You might, in one way or another."

"Not me. I've been arrested six times. You think I don't know how to keep my mouth shut?"

"Lying down in front of a truck is not the same as murder, Jennifer. Both acts leave a mark on you, but the marks are different."

"Let me ask the formal questions," Giles said, "if you don't mind."

"Are you really her boyfriend?" Jennifer's eyes were bright.

"I've been Miss Macintosh's friend and admirer for—"

"Anglos." There was disgust in Jennifer's voice.

"I have known Giles for fifteen years," Isabel said. "Since shortly after his wife's death. He is a wonderful man in every way and I love him very deeply."

"Why don't you marry him, huh? This is my mother asking, you understand? Maybe I'll find out what to tell her."

"I don't think—" Giles said.

"I leveled with you"—Jennifer turned on him fiercely—"and I need an answer. You want to be cold, Anglo; get out."

"I would have married Giles then," Isabel said, "that first year, if he had asked me. He really needed me then. Now? Now he's self-reliant, very. It's too late."

Giles looked surprised. "But—but it was too soon. I didn't know. I was afraid to ask." Then, remembering where he was, he said, "But we'll talk about that later. Let's—Jennifer."

"Yes," Isabel said, "Jennifer. Since I'm not your mother, I can say it. Find someone to take care of, Jenny. A person, not an organization. When you do, you might even have some moments of happiness."

"There aren't any around," Jennifer said simply, "that are worth a damn. And I'm not a lesbian, so that's that."

There was a moment's dead silence, then Giles spoke. "You've been to Professor Humboldt's, Jennifer, and you could probably find your way there again at night. Is that correct?"

Jennifer nodded. "You're in good physical condition, Jennifer; you can ride a bike and jog. Correct?" Jennifer nodded again. "You hated Professor Humboldt, didn't you?"

"Everybody did. He was a racist, militarist, sadistic bastard. I'm glad he's dead, even if it costs me."

"Then why did you work with him? You didn't have to."

"The kids, that's why. So they could read. You don't read, you don't get anywhere. This was a way, a terrific idea, using games, real games, crosswords, to get them to read. I've got hundreds of kids reading now, in only three years, while we were learning how to do it, kids who would never in their life open a book. Kids who, three years ago, would have been ashamed to read, *ashamed*, they go to the library now, by themselves. They want books, can't get enough. And when we give them the week's new puzzles, they brag about how fast they're going to finish. For that I'd work for the devil himself."

"But now that the Project is ready for publication," Giles said, "now that Professor Humboldt is no longer needed..."

"It would have been better if he had been killed three months from now, but we'll manage."

"What about your tenure, Jennifer?" Isabel asked.

"Now that you're taking over, Dean, I'm going to get tenure. You know how good I am and you're not afraid of me."

"Tenure is awarded for scholarship, Jennifer, not sex or minority involvement."

"I did a great job on the Project; read my papers. You can see that the book is published; we don't need Humboldt for that. And I'm a terrific teacher; I've inspired more kids than any three other teachers in the school put together."

"What will you do, Jennifer, if you don't get tenure? Call out the troops?"

"You want me to become a vice-president, is that it? Well, I don't need anybody's help. I'll take the gamble: I'll stay right here for another year and I'll publish till it's coming out of your ears. Good stuff too. But if you do that to me, Dean, the day I get tenure, so help me, I'll quit and go to another school. With tenure. And you can explain that to Jordan."

"You should have become a vice-president, Jennifer," Isabel said. "We'd both have fewer headaches."

"Can we please get on with the murder?" Giles pleaded. "We have another appointment left, Isabel. Remember?"

"I didn't kill him," Jennifer said. "If that's what you want to hear."

"Then who did?" Giles asked. "Why should we take your word for it?"

"Because you don't have any evidence," Jennifer said. "If you had the slightest bit, you would have brought in the cops. You took everybody else's word, I know, and they're all liars and hypocrites—you should have seen them kissing Humboldt's ass—so you might as well take mine. I'm the only one around here who talks straight."

"You didn't answer my question," Giles said. "Who do you think did it?"

"Tinguely, probably. She's been screwing everything in sight for years, so she must have made a play for Humboldt too. When he got tired of her—sooner or later you gotta talk, you know—when he found out what a narcissistic phony she is, he dropped her. She couldn't take that—her ego is all in her looks—so she killed him."

"And the puzzles? The seventh crosswords?"

"To torture him. To tell him his pet Project was going to go down the drain too."

"Do you know something I don't know about Tinguely? Something firm, verifiable?"

"Just common sense."

"If it wasn't Tinguely, who would be your second choice?"

"Karas. She's dying to head the Project herself, be the big shot. With Humboldt out of the way, she'll try to take over. Wait and see."

"Bruce Yablonski thinks he should head the Project now."

"Forget it. None of the men did it. None of them."

"What makes you so sure?"

"No *cojones*. It took a woman. You'll see."

"Zapata," Isabel said, "you're a female chauvinist sow."

"Facts are facts, Dean. I'll accept your public apology in front of the whole Women's Group when you find I'm right."

29

"**Y**OU REALLY SHOULDN'T HAVE DISCUSSED OUR PRIvate affairs with a stranger, Isabel," Giles said. "With anyone, for that matter."

"It was the only way to get her to open up," Isabel said. "But I—I was also talking to you, Giles. I wanted you to know."

"You could have told me later. When we were alone."

"You would have—have reasoned with me, shown me how wrong I was. Illogical. These are my feelings, Giles, not to be reasoned with, right or wrong, not to be thought about, just understood."

"Even if that were true...I never discuss our private affairs with anyone else."

"Does Oliver think we should get married?"

"Of course he— That's different. Oliver is like family, Isabel. He's been with me for forty years. He saved my life twice."

"I know, Giles, I was just explaining, even sort of apologizing for— I do love you."

"Is your independence that important to you, Isabel? I can understand that, and I would not interfere."

"I know you wouldn't, and your saying that shows that you—I didn't explain it well enough. It's nothing that you would do, darling, it's that you would be there, my *husband*. So I'd *want* to do for you, to make you happy, whatever pleased you, even if I didn't really want to do it."

"Don't you do that now? As I do for you? Because I love you?"

"Of course, darling, but I don't have to. That makes all the difference."

They walked quietly together, hand in hand, down the street. "Did you mean that?" he asked.

"About wanting to marry you then?" she asked. He nodded. "Yes, I did. But the time passed, the right time. Maybe I should have told you then."

"I wish you had. We've missed many years of happiness, Isabel."

"The pendulum swings both ways, Giles. What else did we miss?"

"I would have been proud and happy to have you for my wife, Isabel. Even if we'd had problems, we'd have had them together."

"We've been apart together for fifteen years, Giles, and we've shared more happiness than most married couples. I think I made a good trade."

"We could have shared the bad parts too, Isabel, helped each other."

"Bad parts? Do you really want to discuss Zapata now, Giles?"

"I don't, but we should. We have to." Giles took a deep breath. "Did she do it, Isabel? From what you told me before, I had a very different picture of her."

"She's an expert manipulator, Giles. Beware. I don't mean she lied directly, except possibly about killing Humboldt, but the way she presented herself—that was a performance."

"I wondered about that, Isabel. She knew we were coming and she knew exactly when. She could just as easily have left the work, if that's what it was, until after we had left. I can't believe she's such a creature of habit, or so obsessed with duty, or so pressed for time, that it had to be done right then and there."

"A defense mechanism? For the WASPs? The Anglos? It can't have been easy for a skinny little Mexican girl, especially with that name, to grow up in Texas. She had to learn some tricks on the way."

"She seemed at home in the role, Isabel."

"I'm sure it was at least partly true, one of her personae. I wish I knew how much of what she told us was the truth. I wish I knew exactly what she has against her family, why she revolted against her father. It might explain why she hated Humboldt so much."

30

"I KNEW YOU'D BE HUNGRY," EVELYN TINGUELY SAID, "so I prepared a light supper. I hope you don't mind eating in the kitchen." Evelyn's long heavy blond hair was tied with a light-blue satin ribbon and flung over her left shoulder, shimmering with each bounce of her white cotton blouse. She wore a long, pleated navy-blue skirt, under which red slippers played.

"It smells delicious," Isabel said, "but it must have a ton of garlic in it. What is it?"

"Bagna cauda, the perfect hot dip for crisp cold vegetables. Olive oil and butter, mashed anchovies and garlic, heated to just below smoking. I always put extra garlic in when I don't have a date." She caught Isabel's glance at Giles and said, "The next dish has garlic in it, too, but it's all right if you both eat it."

"It really is delicious," Giles said between crunches, "and this is the perfect beer to go with it."

"Priors Double Dark," Evelyn said. "I always keep some in the refrigerator. It's heavy, rich, and somewhat sweet. Very European. Certain kinds of men love it; I use it as a test."

"If they like it, they'll like you?" Giles asked. "I should imagine that anyone you invite to your house must qualify."

"Most men are fakers," Evelyn said primly. "They'll say whatever they think you want to hear just to get invited, and then, when I give them a choice, pick light beer and hamburgers."

"You didn't give us a choice," Giles said.

"I could tell right away that you were the type of man who would appreciate the unusual, the striking, and the intense. Dean Macintosh too."

"What fantastically exotic dish can follow the one before us?" Isabel asked.

"Just cold pasta, Dean. Cold Chinese noodles tossed with sesame oil, soy sauce, chili oil, garlic, a scraping of ginger, and chopped scallions. Try it now. Do you like it?"

"It's delicious," Isabel admitted. "I could live on this forever. Are you a vegetarian, Evelyn?"

"Oh, no. I like to try *everything*. Nothing is too outrageous for me if it promises to be *exciting*." Evelyn was quickly cleaning her plate. "And if I enjoy the new sensation, I *devour* it all."

"You shouldn't have gone to so much trouble," Isabel said.

"It was no trouble at all, Dean," she said. "Less than fifteen minutes. The dessert is just sliced preserved ginger in its own syrup, with some heavy cream floated. And just for you—everybody knows your taste—some shaved bitter chocolate on top."

"I may decide you're innocent right now, Evelyn," Isabel said. "Does everyone who comes up here get the royal treatment?"

"Very few get up here, Dean, rumor notwithstanding. And if he's worth it, I really take the time and trouble to prepare everything properly. *Everything*."

"Do you have an alibi for last night, Evelyn?"

"If you mean did I have a guest here at the time of the murder, the answer is no."

"You were without a date on Saturday night?"

"He seemed so promising when I first met him that—but he turned out to be stupid and a bore. That's an unforgivable combination."

"You mean relatively stupid, don't you?"

"Well, of course. You don't think I'd associate with *ordinary* men, do you? But he was so coarse, a grabber, and all he could talk about was how I looked. I *know* how I look; I want to be *interested*, amused, intrigued. If men would only realize that the most important sex organ is above the eyebrows, *I'd* have more fun too."

"There are still some intelligent ones around, Evelyn. Don't lose faith."

"Oh, I know, I know." She looked directly at Giles. "And when I meet one, I am not afraid to grasp the nettle."

"There's a quotation in which the word after *nettle* is *danger*."

"Shakespeare also said, 'Let me not to the marriage of true minds admit impediment.'"

"There's an even more apt quotation, which begins, 'Art is long, life is short.' It ends with 'and experiment perilous.'"

"May I assure you, Dean, that the most important goal in my life, for the next year at least, is getting tenure."

"I am so relieved to hear that, Dr. Tinguely. When the hormones storm through the races, they can surge above the eyebrows and wreak all kinds of havoc."

"'Men have died from time to time, and worms have eaten them, but not for love.' Women too, Dean; they're too smart to risk death for love."

"Speak in quotations, Doctor; they understand English. It is no kindness to disillusion them."

"If you two have finished plotting against your betters"—Giles glared at Isabel—"can we please get back to the murder?" He smiled at Evelyn. "When did your gentleman friend bring you home, Miss Tinguely?"

"If he were either, Mr. Sullivan, I might have brought

him home. I dropped him at the restaurant at nine o'clock and jogged home alone."

"In dress-up shoes?"

"Anyone with taste carries a bag big enough to hold jogging shoes on a first date."

"Did you go straight home? How long did it take you?"

"First I knocked off Professor Humboldt, then I jogged home. Got there at nine-thirty."

"Did anyone see you?"

"I don't think so. Did anyone say they saw me?"

"Did you leave the house again that night?"

"I didn't want to spoil my image; imagine if Zapata saw me without a man on a Saturday night."

"How did you feel about Professor Humboldt?"

"I respected his intelligence."

"Does that mean you didn't like him?"

"It means that nobody liked him; there'd have to be something wrong with anyone who liked a man like that."

"Did he, uh, like you? You're a very attractive young woman, you know."

"How observant you are, Mr. Sullivan. Unfortunately for Professor Humboldt, his taste ran more to the Rubenesque. Have you noticed how often small men, jockeys for instance, fall for the big women?"

"You sound disappointed, Miss Tinguely."

"It's always comforting to be admired, makes life so much easier. And, conversely, not being admired makes one wonder if, maybe, one is losing her touch."

"You tried?"

"I batted my false eyelashes at him just in case I'd need a mentor one day. No reaction."

"You're a respected scholar," Isabel said. "Don't you find it demeaning to use those tactics?"

"In this world," Evelyn said, "you use everything you've got. You'd be surprised how many supposedly disinterested *women*, professors and administrators, have downgraded me. Out of fear? Envy? What? You tell me, Dean."

"The herd fears the predator, Doctor. The mediocre

hate the superior. You're a sociologist; you should know that."

"But why should another predator fear me? Dean?"

"Some woods are overhunted; there isn't enough prey to go around," Isabel said. "Could you find Professor Humboldt's cabin in the dark?"

"Probably. Couldn't anyone who's been there a few times?"

"Probably. I'm sure I could, Evelyn. Did you kill Humboldt?"

"No. I never kill single heterosexual males; they should be a protected species."

"What about the crosswords?" Giles broke in. "The seventh puzzles?"

"The professor was upset by them," Evelyn said. "All out of proportion to the fact, I thought."

"Didn't you, all of you, find a message in the extra puzzles that indicated that Humboldt was a fugitive Nazi?"

"It was Bruce's idea to treat the puzzles as a single entity. We abstracted the words that fit, very closely, the picture of a Nazi torturer."

"Are you sure that's the correct message? Isn't it possible that another message could be found in the puzzles?"

"You're welcome to try, Mr. Sullivan. When you leave I'll give you a copy of my solved puzzles and the message. If you pick only a few words, yes, you can get almost anything out of that many words, but we have nineteen words put together in a rational pattern. That gives it a very high probability."

"Do you think, Miss Tinguely, that Professor Humboldt was Nazi?"

"He was Nazi-like in some ways, but I find it hard to believe he was the person described in the message. There *is* a connection. I'm sure of that. Why would he be so upset otherwise?"

"Your colleagues believe that Professor Humboldt's murderer constructed the puzzles. Do you agree?"

"Probably. Who else would it have been, Mr. Sullivan?"

"They also believe that the killer is one of you six. Do you agree with that too?"

"I suppose so, but it's just a hunch. Plus the crossword connection, of course."

"Which one was it, Miss Tinguely?"

"There's nothing definite...."

"Which one, Miss Tinguely?" Giles stared unblinkingly into her eyes.

Evelyn looked away. "Carl Richter, most likely. He's very short-tempered."

"You think it was a crime of passion?"

"It didn't have to be that, Mr. Sullivan. Maybe when he confronted the professor... He hadn't intended to kill him but something was said, done, something that drove Carl—"

Isabel stood up abruptly. "Let's go home, Giles; we've learned all we have to here. We must relax, rest for a while, digest what we've learned today. I'll get the puzzles from Evelyn and meet you outside. I want to discuss some school matters with Dr. Tinguely."

As soon as Giles left, Isabel said, "I'm going to be on all six tenure committees, Evelyn, and I'm probably going to take over the Project."

"I know; Bruce phoned me."

"Trying to unite you all against me?"

"He felt we could do it ourselves."

"And get tenure? You think you can get it without me?"

"I could try publishing like crazy next year, but I'd rather do it with you on my side, Dean."

"I'm not supposed to be on anyone's side, Evelyn."

"May I *reassure* you, Dean, that I would sacrifice anything for tenure?"

31

"DON'T YOU FIND MISS TINGUELY A VERY ATTRACTIVE woman, Isabel?"

"Don't be fooled by her looks, Sullivan; she really is a beautiful woman."

"I'm not sure I—"

"Don't bother, Sullivan. Just force your eyes back into your head and keep walking."

"Did you notice, Isabel, how she looked in her at-home clothes? She looked better—*sexier* is the word—in that simple dress than Virginia Wagner did in her French Maid's costume."

"You noticed that, did you, Sullivan? I wonder why. Maybe she got it at the same mail order house that— forget it. No, don't forget it; let me teach you something. She was wearing her homebody costume like Marie Antoinette and her court dressed as milkmaids. Tinguely's no more a homemaker than Marie A. was a milkmaid. This was, in case you hadn't noticed, the good old red, white, and blue. And Blond. A color scheme to strike the heart of every red-blooded American boy. And it worked on you, you—you amateur."

"But she really cooked. It was a great meal, wasn't it?"

"Sure, but did you notice something? Any woman would have, but she doesn't care about that. These were all simple things to make. The bagna cauda? Mash up some anchovies, spoon pre-chopped garlic in oil over it, turn on the heat, and presto, instant ecstasy. The sesame noodles? Pour on the oils and spices, mix, and serve. You can even buy frozen chopped scallions. The ginger? Open the jar, slice the roots, pour on cream, shave chocolate, and another man bites the dust. I don't think it took even the fifteen minutes she said."

"But it was delicious, wasn't it?"

"Sure. Sugar and spice. Spectacular. The test is, can she make good scrambled eggs? Bake a good sponge cake? Simple boiled beef? Hah!"

"Relax, Isabel. I'm not going to marry her. I swear."

"If I hadn't been there to protect you, you'd have been proposing by Sunday. She's probably a good—make that an *expert*—lay too."

"She's also intelligent, Isabel. Why are you so hard on her?"

"The easiest way to show a man you're intelligent is to tell him that *he's* intelligent. And that you just lo-o-ve intelligent men."

"You don't like her, do you, Isabel?"

"Not particularly. As a matter of fact, I don't like any of them. I was looking forward so to this weekend, and they ruined it. I haven't had enough sleep. I've been running around all day. My career may be ruined already. The school will suffer no matter what. Whoever did it, I could kill him myself."

"Do you think she did it, Isabel? I don't see—"

"You don't see because you're blinded by golden hair. Your glands are pumping your blood full of—but it won't mean a thing to me tonight. You think I don't know you'll be thinking of her? You can't help it—I know that—but that doesn't make me feel any better. Of course she could have done it; she's almost as smart as Bruce, she's as amoral as Jennifer, and she'd kill to get tenure."

"But did she do it, Isabel?"

"How the hell should I know? But she does *not* get crossed off *my* list."

▨▨▨▨▨▨▨▨▨▨▨▨▨ 32 ◆◆◆

"**O**LIVER SOLVED THE PUZZLES WHILE WE WERE WAITing," Agatha said. "I'll make some cocoa."

"They were not very difficult, sir," Oliver said, "and not very interesting either, except for a few clues here and there. May I ask how you fared?"

"Complete bust," Isabel said, sinking into the kitchen chair and leaning her elbows on the table. "Not a clue in the whole crew."

"Oh, I don't know," Giles said. "We learned a lot about the character of each suspect."

"Character? Is that what it's called? I bet you could give us Evelyn's measurements to the millimeter, including inside seam." Isabel looked contrite. "I'm sorry, Giles. It's just that I feel so beaten. What we learned"—she addressed Agatha and Oliver—"was that each one hated Humboldt, had no alibi, and could easily have gone to Humboldt's house and back without being seen. Motive and opportunity. Means? A hundred means were hanging on Humboldt's wall, just waiting to be used."

"What about the police, Miss Parrot?" Giles asked.

"Have your sources learned anything about what the police found out?"

"Everything," Agatha said. "In one word, nothing. They don't even know about the puzzles yet."

"Why don't we examine the message?" Giles asked. "Here's the list and here's the connected sentence Bruce Yablonski put together. It seems to make a good deal of sense."

"There are even more words he might have used," Oliver said, "'Rip,' 'pus,' 'tie,' 'sheared,' 'The Police,' 'rec,' which might stand for *wreck*, 'acrid,' 'Power,' 'undo,' 'stun,' 'Empire'—*Das Dritte Reich* means The Third Empire—'ices,' which is slang for *kills*, 'tore,' 'obit'—that's, let me see, fourteen more words that could have been fitted in. An impressive number."

"You're not helping, Oliver," Giles said. "You're pointing out what I had already suspected: that the message is not necessarily accurate."

"If you say so, sir." Oliver's face was bland.

"Look at the distribution," Giles said, taking a pen from his pocket, "of the original words Bruce selected. Six from the first puzzle: *Mila*, 'medulla,' 'anon,' *Rache*, 'unfit,' and 'electro.' Then eight words from the second puzzle and five words from the third. But Bruce's sentence combined only the words from the first two puzzles. The words from the third puzzle don't add anything."

"Then why was there a third puzzle?" Agatha asked.

"Precisely. But, more important, Professor Humboldt called in Professor Karas and gave her hell, to quote Virginia Wagner, after the *first* puzzle. What was in that first puzzle to anger him? Or to frighten him? Look at the six words: *Mila, medulla, anon, Rache, unfit,* and *electro.* How can they be put together to give a rational message?"

They all bent over the paper. After a moment Isabel said, "I don't see any combination that makes sense."

"Neither do I," Giles said. "Which leaves only one conclusion: there must be a different message."

"Maybe Bruce was right," Isabel said. "The fact that the crosswords were sent at all is the message."

"I can't accept that," Giles said. "For the amount of

154

time and effort that went into constructing and delivering the puzzles, I'm sure some easier means could have been found to let Humboldt know that someone was threatening the Project. No, there is a message in the crosswords themselves; we just haven't found it yet."

"I had come to that conclusion myself, sir," Oliver said. "However, Agatha and I have been trying for several hours, while we were waiting for your return, and we were unable to extract a useful message either from the individual puzzles or as a group."

"I am certain there is a message there," Giles said.

"Humboldt was an expert puzzle solver," Isabel said. "Maybe the message is deeply concealed. As an acrostic, perhaps?"

"I thought of that, and I've been checking as we were talking," Giles said. "I don't see any combination offhand. Do any of you see anything unusual? Regardless of whether or not it makes a message?"

"I'm not a real puzzle expert," Agatha said, "but I noticed that some of the definitions have question marks at the end. Is that what you mean by unusual?"

"Not at all," Giles said. "A question mark after a clue is the conventional signal from the constructor that the clue is a cryptic, not a straight definition. It's usually a pun or an anagram or a joke. Look at 52 Across, in puzzle two. The definition is 'blanch mink?' a play on words for 'ranch mink.' The light, that is, the word in the puzzle, is 'scald fur,' which is a humorous way of putting it."

"Sorry," Agatha said. "I just thought it might be important because there are six question-marked definitions in the first and second puzzles, and seven in the third."

"What? Six and six? And seven in the last?" Giles got excited. "That's very interesting, Agatha. That may be— In breaking codes it's very significant—it's my hobby," he added hastily, "it's of major importance to find regularities. This could represent a six-word message in each puzzle with a signature in the last one. Let's look at the lights."

"What are lights again, Mr. Sullivan?"

"They're the words, the answers to the clues, in a

crossword, what you write into the blank spaces. From puzzle one we have 'an ounce,' 'inn riding,' 'sheared,' 'bye y'all,' 'pro seeds,' and 'U. Ill.'"

"That doesn't look very promising," Isabel said.

"Maybe they have to be combined. Let's try the second puzzle. 'Two on a hand,' 'scald fur,' 'con tracked,' 'shake,' 'a media,' and 'dancer.'"

"That's not much help either, Giles."

"Here's the third puzzle. 'Writhing,' 'thesis,' 'or 1's,' 'duty,' 'bekilt,' 'lashtime,' and 'ether.'" Giles's face sagged. "Nothing much here either. Well, it sounded like a good approach."

"What if you mixed them?" Agatha asked. "All the puzzles together?"

"I was doing that mentally as I was writing the words down. There's nothing there."

"Look," Isabel said, "we're all tired. Let's drop it for the rest of the evening and relax. We'll try again tomorrow. Who knows what a fresh mind will come up with?"

"You're right, Miss Macintosh," Agatha said. "I'll lead Oliver back. We'll all go to bed early and meet in your office before school opens, say at seven, and go over the puzzles again." Agatha stood up and addressed Isabel. "I heard what you said before, clearly. Don't worry. I'll have my sources keep a sharp eye on Tingly Evelyn."

Giles twitched. "What did you say? Tingly? Is that her name? Write it out for me. Now." Isabel spelled it as she wrote. "T-i-n-g-u-e-l-y. Just like the famous artist, although she's no relation."

"But you pronounced it 'Tong-Wa-Lee.'" Giles looked excited. "Before I met her I thought she was Chinese."

"That's the way she wants it pronounced," Isabel said. "Nothing wrong with that."

"But Agatha called her *Tingly*. As in 'tingle.'"

"That's what I always call her," Agatha said. "Just not to her face. It sort of fits the way she works. Did you ever see her pass through a bunch of men? Like a magnet in a pin factory."

"That's the key; don't you see? Tong-Wa-Lee is Tingly. Now look at the words in the puzzles, the words with the question marks. I mean, don't look; say them. Sound them out. You get a completely different meaning. That's the solution. The message is contained in the *sound* of the words. We cruciverbalists are so used to *seeing* the words that we never say them. The biggest insult in the club is that you move your lips when you read."

"I still don't see a message," Isabel said.

"Yes, you do. It's there. Look at the words in the first puzzle. 'An ounce' has to be 'announce.' 'Inn riding' is 'in writing.' Don't you see? 'Pro seeds' is clearly 'proceeds,' and 'U. Ill.' is 'you will.' 'Sheared' is 'shared,' and 'bye y'all' is 'by all.' The message of the first puzzle is 'You will announce, in writing, (that the) proceeds (be) shared by all.' It's perfect."

"No wonder Humboldt was upset," Isabel said. "Whatever deal he was working on, the constructor wanted the money—what else could 'proceeds' be?—shared by all the participants. Evidently Humboldt had intended to keep everything himself."

"Exactly. Now let's look at the second puzzle," Giles said. "With a little work, now that we know the technique, it becomes clear. 'A media dancer' becomes—say it out loud—'immediate answer.' 'Scald fur' becomes 'is called for,' and 'two on a hand,' and 'shake,' is 'to honor handshake.' 'Con tracked' is, of course, 'contract.' '(An) immediate answer is called for to honor (our) handshake contract.'"

"So now we know," Isabel said, "that there was no written contract between Humboldt and the puzzle constructor. That's why he used this means of pushing Humboldt to keep his word."

"There is much more revealed than that, Isabel, by these messages; we'll examine that later. Look at the third puzzle. Put it in this order and say it aloud. 'Thesis lashtime ether duty writhing or l's bekilt.' 'This is (the) last time; either do the right thing or else be killed.' That proves the puzzle constructor is the murderer."

"We all knew that," Isabel said.

"We assumed it," Giles corrected. "Now we know. There's a lot here to think about."

"Can't you do your thinking tomorrow morning?" Isabel asked. "It's after nine and we've been running around all day. Enough is enough. I want to go to bed."

"You're right, Dean," Agatha said. "Time to go home. We'll meet at the office at seven. Come, Oliver." She got up to go. "One more thing, Mr. Sullivan," she said. "Doesn't it also prove that one of the six professors in the Project group is the killer?"

"Not conclusively," Giles said, "but it's fairly obvious."

"Yes," Isabel said, "but which one?"

 33

"THERE ARE MANY THINGS WE CAN DEDUCE FROM THE messages," Giles said from his straight chair next to Isabel's desk.

"The first thing is that the constructor of the puzzles is very bright," Isabel said. "I don't know the history of crosswords as well as you, Giles, but I do think this is an entirely new form. Putting a message into a crossword is old hat, but I'm sure it's definitely novel to use cryptics to provide lights which must be *spoken* to be converted into the correct words which can then be assembled into a message."

"Could something like that be patented?" Agatha asked. "There might be money in that."

"It would take several thousand dollars," Giles said, "and several years to accomplish, if it could be done at all. The name could be copyrighted, however. 'Crossorals,' or 'Auralcross,' 'Acousticross,' 'Soundlikes,' some combination indicating crosswords and sound. What this does show is that the killer needed money now, not three years from now."

159

"Bright and needs money now?" Isabel said. "That covers all six."

"But where is there any money in what they were doing?" Agatha asked.

"How about the Project book?" Giles asked.

"Forget it," Isabel said. "Do you know how much a scholarly book gets as an advance? About as much as a short article for a slick magazine."

"Aren't there royalties?"

"A few hundred a year, of which Humboldt was to get half and the other six one-twelfth each. Not enough to kill over."

"Couldn't there be a popular book in this, Isabel?"

"How many copies would you buy, Giles, of a book that describes how to devise crosswords to help people learn to read? One for the club library, perhaps? Now, if you could find a way to combine sex and violence with crosswords, that might become a best seller."

"There has to be sizable money in it somewhere," Giles persisted. "Don't forget what the messages said, that the proceeds were to be shared by all. That means that the murderer wanted a one-twelfth share of something, and that had to be enough to kill over."

"You're talking big money there, Giles. Poor as they are, none of the six are going to kill for, say, ten thousand dollars. If we assume that as little as twenty-five thousand, barely enough for a professor to live on for a year, is a twelfth share, there has to be three hundred thousand dollars involved. In the Project? From crosswords? Impossible."

"Maybe it's money combined with something else," Agatha said. "Tenure, for instance."

"That doesn't fit the facts," Giles said. "The constructor went to considerable trouble to stay incognito, sacrificed a lot of money. If he thought he could have gotten the money while revealing himself, which he would have to do to get tenure, too, why didn't he ask for half? All?"

"That's not logical either," Isabel said. "After the last puzzle he went to Humboldt's cabin. There he had to reveal himself. Why did he go? If he intended to kill Humboldt, why not bring a weapon? Or waylay Humboldt in the wood? Or sneak into the house just before Virginia Wagner came, hide until she left, and then kill Humboldt? The body wouldn't have been found until Monday, at least. That would blur the time of the killing and make an alibi possible. What he did, the way he did it, insured that the body would be found within minutes of the murder. So he knew that if he revealed himself, he would either gain everything he wanted, or Humboldt *could* not tell on him."

"The killer had to have a very simple demand," Giles said, "whatever it was, that Humboldt could agree to immediately. If Humboldt agreed, whatever reprisals he might take against the now-known killer would be worth the loss to the killer. The gain, the killer's need, must have been very great for that. Humboldt could not only throw the killer off the Project; he could guarantee that the killer would not get tenure."

"Maybe the killer had an ongoing hold over Humboldt," Agatha suggested.

"Then there would be no need to kill Humboldt," Giles said. "No, it had to be as I described. When Humboldt refused the killer's demand, the killer had to murder Humboldt, as he had threatened in the message of the last puzzle, to prevent his being thrown off the Project and being deprived of tenure."

"So the purpose of the messages in the puzzles," Isabel said, "was to make Humboldt announce in writing that the prize, whatever it was, would be shared by *all six professors* without ever revealing to anyone who the killer was, or even revealing to his colleagues that any pressure had been applied to Humboldt. It was only when Humboldt refused that it became necessary to face him and to give him one last chance to agree. The killer knew the risk, was willing to take it, and really expected Humboldt to agree. That's why he didn't bring a weapon."

"Or decided not to use his weapon," Giles said, "because it increased his risk."

"I doubt that," Isabel said. "The killer must have been fairly sure Humboldt would agree. After all, there was a handshake contract. He knew that there were a hundred weapons available to choose from and also knew that Humboldt would not resist him."

"How could he know that?" Agatha asked.

"I don't know that yet," Isabel said, "but we'll find out. It is clear that Humboldt was sitting calmly in his chair when he was stabbed."

"We are now sure," Giles said, "that the killer knew Humboldt's habits, including Virginia Wagner; that the killer knew of a large amount of money Humboldt had made a handshake contract about with the six professors, although the other five didn't seem to know about it."

"Maybe they all did," Agatha said, "and are keeping quiet to protect their shares."

"If that's the case, they're all doing a good job concealing it," Isabel said. "Virginia Wagner didn't mention any large amounts of money, and she handled all of Humboldt's communications."

"Maybe the prize wasn't monetary," Giles said. "Maybe it was a prize such as the Nobel or Pulitzer."

"Not very likely for something like teaching by crosswords," Isabel said. "The Liberman Prize is prestigious and pays ten thousand dollars, but they all know about that. What do we do now, Giles?"

"Find out which of the six is the killer," he replied. "And I think I know how to do it. Last night, when you accused me of thinking—inappropriate thoughts, I wasn't. I had just thought of a way, a *possible* way, of finding the killer."

"I knew there was something wrong," Isabel said. "And what makes you think, Sullivan, that thinking about the murder was any less appropriate than—than any other inappropriate thoughts?"

"I wasn't thinking; it came in a flash. I couldn't help it."

"Typical childish male excuse. I take it, it won't happen again?"

"It doesn't have to, Isabel, anymore. Now, what I'd like you to do is arrange a meeting of the six professors, their usual time and place—three o'clock, wasn't it?—to have another crossword session. Can you do it?"

"Of course. They'll jump through hoops for me now. What do I do there?"

"Give them a crossword to solve. Follow my directions exactly. As soon as I finish something at the library—you can get me in, can't you?—I'll construct the puzzle."

"Just because it worked once? Are you sure it will work again, Giles?"

"No, Isabel, but it's our only chance. If this doesn't work, there's nothing left."

34

"**I** DON'T WANT TO HEAR ANY MORE ARGUMENTS," Isabel said firmly. "You can either stay and follow my directions exactly or walk out now. You're not glued to the chair."

"That's not much of a choice, Dean," Bruce Yablonski said. "You control the funds for the Project, you said you would take over Professor Humboldt's position in the Project, and you have a great deal of influence on our tenure."

"There is no threat here. If I have to make decisions regarding your effectiveness in the Project in lieu of publication, and if I have decisions to make on your worthiness for tenure, I have to base them on something. One of these things is the crossword puzzle I placed on your desk, upside down. The better you do on this test, the more likely I am to consider you worthy. Any questions?"

"Same conditions as our usual session?" Carl Richter asked.

"Razor-point pens; blue for the lights, red for a correction. A second correction flunks you. I want to emphasize that the number of blanks counts very heavily, and the number of mistakes counts just as heavily, both against you. Further, you have to use your judgment as to how long you want to struggle over a word you can't get. Speed counts *very* heavily. First done is very good; last done is very bad. Yes, you're competing against one another. One difference: I'll be holding the stopwatch. When I say Go, turn over your paper and start. As soon as you've finished, hand me your sheet and leave. Ready? GO!"

ACROSS

1 Indy player
5 Get a grip on
10 Binges
14 Colorful deep-sea fish
15 Mailman's itinerary
16 ___ pricing
17 Dam
18 Square-dance group, e.g.
19 Catch 40
20 Barn creature, of the non-
  hooting variety
22 Eat at
23 Benevolent, protective
  one
24 Unsurpassable
26 Pit
29 Pitching tactic
31 Be below par
34 Jetsetter's summer place
35 Significant
37 Lily plant

38 Sooner born
39 Cauldron concoction
40 Unlikely to let up
42 "___ but known . . ."
43 Prado stuff
44 Is impending
45 Is impending
46 Mild-mannered reporter
47 Beethoven's "___ Elise"
48 Two-edged Maori club
51 Tale of woe
57 African timber trees
58 Half a *Star Wars* name
59 Dusseldorf duck
60 Roman arrow launcher
61 Russian Turk
62 Sentential essential
63 Hindu groom's shackle
64 Antelope of Africa
65 Annoying person

DOWN

1 Where's the beef?
2 Oilmen's org.
3 Den
4 The Andrews Sisters, e.g.
5 Break down
6 Nessie's home, e.g.
7 Indy entry
8 Airline staffer
9 ASPCA folks
10 Arbiter
11 In due course
12 Nile city
13 Lather
21 Stately shade
25 Saul's uncle
26 Bow of film fame
27 Boss, at times
28 Porno patron
29 Ancillary

30 Short of
31 Presidential middle name
32 ___ France
33 *Hardly Working* star
35 Ruler
36 Repulsive
41 22½°
45 Snooker stick
46 Gurkha's weapon
47 Interslope inlet
48 Antitank gun
49 Weapon of the Roman
  Empire
50 Sword: archaic
52 "___ boy!"
53 Horse of another color?
54 Be sure of
55 Seamstress's kit
56 Dollars for quarters

SULLIVAN'S TEST

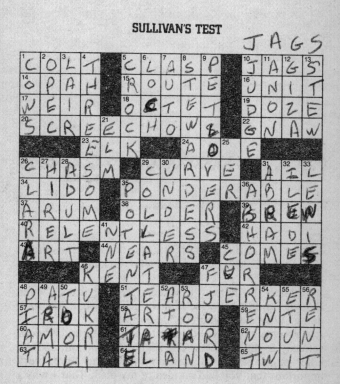

 **35**

GILES SPREAD THE SIX SHEETS OUT ON AGATHA'S kitchen table. "No doubt about who the killer is, is there, Isabel?"

"I knew the moment I looked at it," Isabel said, "even though I didn't have the faintest idea of what you were doing. Why didn't you confide in me?"

"You might have transmitted something subconsciously to the suspects. The slightest suspicion, and the killer might have... It was a very tenuous thing, very important that you had no idea of my plan. That's why I asked you not to look at the front of the puzzles until everyone had left."

"I understand that now, Giles, but when you wouldn't confide in me, I was ready to—to excommunicate you. I'm not a zombie, you know."

"I know, Isabel, I really know. Now, Agatha, please pick out the killer's crossword."

"It's this one, Mr. Sullivan," she said without hesitation, "but you've taped over the killer's name."

"That was the final check, Agatha. Thank you."

"It was easy, Mr. Sullivan, even though I don't know all that much about crosswords. But what does *kukri* mean?"

"It's the proper name for the Gurkha knife, Agatha. Very few people, in America at least, have ever heard that word. It's a fearsome weapon in the hands of an expert. There was a picture in the book of a Gurkha cutting the head off a bullock with a single blow of his kukri. Please don't discuss this with anyone; that's very important. Don't even mention that Professor Humboldt was stabbed. I'm sure that's one of the things the police are keeping secret."

"Anyone could have gotten the 'K,'" Isabel said, "the first letter of kukri, from the crossing words."

"Of course," Giles said, "that's the beauty of it; I designed it that way. You have the first letter of the word that leads into the lower left-hand corner, but you don't know the rest of the word unless you know kukri."

"Couldn't you build up kukri from the rest of the words in that corner?" Isabel asked.

"Never. Impossible. Especially without references. I put in the most obscure words I could find that related to weapons. I doubt that even Professor Humboldt could have filled in a single word in that corner without a library at his disposal. The only way the killer could get the first word is if he *knew* what a kukri was."

"That puzzle," Isabel said, "it's not a very elegant construction, Giles. Only six of the highly obscure words that fill the lower left corner concern weapons. In a really super classic puzzle, all eight words would not only have been highly obscure but would have described *modern* weapons."

"Are you crazy, Isabel? Do you know how hard it was to get six out of eight? It's impossible to get all eight. I guarantee it. I defy anyone to fill that whole corner with highly obscure words for modern weapons."

"Hannibal could have done it," Isabel said, careful not to smile. "You just don't have the touch, Giles. Sorry. But I'll overlook your inadequacies, Sullivan, if you'll keep your mind on your work in the future. No more inappropriate thoughts, agreed?"

Giles sighed, and agreed. "Good." Isabel sounded satisfied. "Forgiven. Now, I must tell you, darling, there's a slight flaw in your operations. How do you get evidence to convict the killer? Or even to prove to a grand jury who the killer is?"

"You don't. It's impossible."

"What about kukri in the puzzle?"

"That isn't evidence. Do you think it would have been written in if it were?"

"You mean all—everything we did is wasted? Useless?"

"Not at all. At least we've learned—"

"Maybe the police have something by now," Isabel said, turning to Agatha. "What do your sources say?"

"As of last night," Agatha said, "nothing new. No fingerprints, no footprints, no hair, no fibers, no witnesses, no nothing."

"I didn't think they would," Giles said. "This is a very clever killer we're dealing with."

"We can't even stop the killer from benefitting from the murder? Is that what you're telling me, Giles?"

"Well, I—yes. I'm afraid so. There was something, I think, something Virginia Wagner said that didn't register at the time, because there was nothing wrong with it then. But now it irritates me, like a pebble in my shoe. If only—"

"Why not just ask Virginia? The same questions again, I mean?"

"Even if I could remember the exact questions, it wouldn't help. If it was in answer to any direct question I asked, I would have remembered it; that I know. It must have been in a passing remark, an aside. I'll just wait until it comes back to me. Meanwhile I have a plan: I'm going to construct another puzzle."

"Another crossword? Whatever for? We already know—"

"No, no, Isabel. Not for information, for action. It will

also help—not much, but a little—combined with today's puzzle, as corroboration, to show others who the killer is."

"Corroboration? Not evidence?"

"Sorry, Isabel. That's the way it is. I don't believe there is any evidence we can possibly get that will be admissible in court. But that doesn't mean we're completely helpless."

"It sure sounds like it to me. What do you want me to do?"

"Get Virginia Wagner to let me examine Humboldt's files; maybe it will help refresh my memory. Then I want you to give each of our six suspects a copy of the puzzle I'm going to construct."

"Another test? And why all six? We know who—"

"So as not to warn the killer. And this is a take-home test. Make six copies of the puzzle. Give a copy to each of the six first thing tomorrow morning, say at nine. Same rules as before, but speed is not important. The puzzles must be returned, completed, to you personally, at your office at, let's say, five o'clock tomorrow afternoon."

"That's all?"

"That's all. I'll do the rest."

"What rest?"

"Just routine; it doesn't concern you. With a little luck—"

"Anything you do, Giles, concerns me."

"Really, Isabel. Routine. You will be doing your part by giving out the puzzles in the morning and collecting them in the afternoon. Just don't leave the office until you have all six completed puzzles."

"Whatever you say, Giles." Agatha observed Isabel's highly uncharacteristic surrender suspiciously, but said nothing.

ACROSS

1 Streetcar
5 "... once through ____ halls"
10 Kenobi and company
14 Migratory worker
15 Make one's day
16 *Metamorphoses* man
17 Dreaded fellow?
18 Bugs's Nimrod
19 Part of *SNL*
20 "____ Edmonton," '83 Stanley Cup headline?
22 Country homes
24 Marseilles moo-juice
25 Antimacassar
26 Cotton Club milieu
29 Velvety surface
30 C&W or R&B
33 Columbus's home
34 Chews the scenery
36 AFB in Colorado
37 Know in one's bones
39 Art medium
40 Pe-qoph link
42 Hardly a Derby winner
43 "Neckties"
46 Aid for Holmes
47 Half a musical
48 Staircase descender
49 Played the pest
51 Soaks flax
52 Croat's neighbor
53 The Bohemian commercial?
56 Illegible, maybe
60 Bookkeeping woes
61 "____ River"
63 Neighborhood
64 Sharon's co-star
65 Mini egg
66 Maugham opus
67 Actress Moran
68 Churchly goings-on
69 Lectern

DOWN

1 Tak resident
2 Aligned array
3 Magwitch of *Great Expectations*
4 Sour cherries
5 Fore o'clock?
6 Ration out
7 Cloverleaf feature
8 Had a ham
9 Abject
10 Very, in Merrie Olde
11 Exorcist's foe
12 Met star, maybe
13 Mid-March
21 Return-mail requisite: Abbr.
23 That is for Brutus
25 Cover information
26 Anwar's successor
27 Winning for the nonce
28 One-fourth of the Fab Four
29 Beauty queen's sine qua non
30 Quotidian trio
31 Excessive
32 Silver or Scout
35 Love and hate
38 Nine, in combinations
41 Poet who won't strike?
44 Alfresco
45 Novelist Laurence and family
50 Area near SE Mass.
51 Up
52 Go up
53 Somewhat, with "a"
54 Time seemingly decayed?
55 Actor *né* Weisenfreund
56 X-rated stuff

57 Highland hillside
58 Mainlanders' mementos

59 W.W.II GIs' newspaper
62 VII x VIII

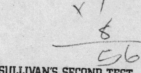

SULLIVAN'S SECOND TEST

173

36

GILES CAREFULLY CUT THE POLICE SEAL ON HUM-
boldt's front door and went to work on the lock. Not
having Oliver's skill, it took him two full minutes to find
the appropriate pins to push up while keeping the cylinder
under tension, but finally the lock yielded.

When Isabel tapped him on the shoulder he wheeled
around fast, the sword halfway out of his cane. "Oh, my
God, Isabel, don't ever do that again. I thought it was—
What are you doing here?" He pushed the saber back and
twisted the cane closed. "You're supposed to be—"

"You tell me, Sullivan, to make six copies of a secret
crossword puzzle guaranteed to trap the evil killer, and
you expect me not to make a copy for myself?"

"But I told you to stay in your office until five to collect
the completed crosswords. That was very important."

"Bullshit, Sullivan. The killer isn't going to bring in
any puzzle, and you know it. The killer is coming here
in one hour. Or less. You think I didn't solve the puzzle?
Or interpret the message? I also went to Humboldt's office
while you were constructing the puzzle. Virginia Wagner

showed me the file you looked at. I read the letters and came to the same conclusion you did. Now let's get inside, fast."

"No. Certainly not. It's too dangerous."

"Is this Sullivan, the lying rat, who told me it was just routine?"

"It is a common practice. If you know anything about police techniques."

"I read whodunits, Sullivan, and I know all about tethered goats as bait for tigers, and about recorded confessions. They only work in fiction; poor fiction, at that. I'm going inside. You can stay here if you want to."

"Wait. All right. I didn't want you to get involved. It could be somewhat dangerous, that is, routinely dangerous, and I didn't want you to— I'd die before I allowed anyone to hurt you, Isabel."

"I appreciate your feeling, but can't you see it's insulting too? I'm a big girl, Giles, competent and respected in my field. And this is my turf."

"Yes. Admitted. But this work is my work."

"The job goes to whoever can do it, Sullivan. The killer takes one look at you sitting behind that desk, and all bets are off. And what would you offer? What carrot? What stick? 'If you confess, I'll ask Miss Macintosh to grant you tenure.' It won't work, Giles; only I can carry it off."

"I don't care. *I'm* going into the study. *I* will be sitting behind that desk. *You* can't stop me, Isabel."

"Of course not, you great big muscular brute. There's nothing poor little me can do, is there? I'll just go outside like a good little girl, and hang around the front door, whimpering."

Giles looked at her carefully, studied her, and saw that, as always, he could not defeat this determined woman, this wonderful woman who, unfortunately, was, in this case at least, absolutely right. "Very well, then. You sit behind the desk. You know what has to be done. But I'll be nearby, just in case. And Isabel, please don't—it isn't worth it. I'd rather a hundred killers . . ."

She put her arms around him and held him tightly to

herself. "I'll be careful, darling. I do love you, too, and part of me is very happy, and very proud, that you want to protect me. I hope it won't be necessary, but if it is, I'd rather depend on you for my life than on anyone else in the world."

She walked into Fabian Humboldt's dark, windowless study, turned on the shaded reading lamp to cast a cone of light directly on the center of the desk, and pulled it even lower so that the chair behind the desk was in partial darkness. She carefully did not look into the dark corners of the long room. Isabel selected a big thick book on castle architecture from the shelves behind the desk. She sat at the desk, opposite the wall of knives, in the big wing chair in which Fabian Humboldt had been murdered, opened the book, and waited.

37

"YOU SENT FOR ME, DEAN?"

"Ah, yes," Isabel said, laying the big book flat. "I didn't hear you come in; running shoes make very little noise. Won't you sit down?"

"Thank you, no, Dean. I'm on a tight schedule and can't stay very long. The message was *Mimi ad scabbard tee time awer isles top 10 yr.*, which translates into 'Meet me at the scabbard at tea time or I'll stop your tenure.' It took me a while to figure out that 'scabbard' is the place where swords are kept; Professor Humboldt's study."

"I knew you'd figure it out, Karen; you're the smartest of the lot."

"Thank you, Dean. I've always admired you too. What was so important that you wanted to talk to me about that you had to threaten to stop my tenure? A simple invitation would have brought me to your office. Why here?"

"Won't you, at least, take off your cap and gloves, Karen? And your dark glasses. The light here is poor enough as it is."

"I'm comfortable the way I am, Dean, but I will take off my sunglasses. What can I do for you?"

"If you want to rush things, you can go with me to the police and confess that you killed Professor Humboldt."

"Why should I do a thing like that, Dean? I didn't kill him."

"Oh, come now, Karen, you solved the last puzzle. That's why you're here."

"If you'll point out where the microphone is, Dean, I'll talk clearly into it."

Isabel shook her head. "There really is no tape recorder going, Karen."

"No matter. Are you saying that because I had a flash of insight and figured out the message in the puzzle you handed out this morning I killed Professor Humboldt? I don't see the connection."

"Don't fence with me, Karen. The message was concealed in today's puzzle by the same technique used in the three seventh puzzles."

"How interesting, Dean. When I get home I must check those puzzles and see what the messages are."

"You invented a new type of crossword, Karen. Why didn't you capitalize on it?"

"Really, Dean? I may just do that one day, when I have the money, if no one else claims authorship. Of course, if the real constructor shows up, he'd own all the rights. Still, I don't suppose that will ever happen, since you're acting as though there is a connection between the messages in the crosswords and Professor Humboldt's death."

"The test puzzle that I gave out yesterday was designed so that *no one* could fill in the lower left-hand corner except possibly an expert on obscure weapons, such as Professor Humboldt. The two non-weapons words were so obscure that not one crosswords expert in a million could have known them, especially without references. It was easy to get the first letter of the lead-in word to that corner, *K*. Did you think it referred to you?"

"Everybody calls me K.K., so I automatically assume that any K refers to me."

"Even given the first letter, it would have been impossible to build up that lead-in word from the other words in that field. You filled it in, though you must have hesitated for a moment, because you wanted to be first and get tenure, because you knew it was worthless as evidence, and because the letter *K* indicated that we already knew it was you. You were the only one of the six, Karen, who knew what a kukri was."

"One tends to pick up odds and ends of knowledge here and there."

"As soon as I knew for sure that it was you, Karen, a lot of things began falling into place. You didn't have an alibi and you were out of the house jogging between nine and eleven. Were you wearing the same dark outfit then as you're wearing now?"

"All except the sunglasses, Dean. It was a dark night."

"I began thinking, Karen, how difficult it would be to jog, or even to walk, through the wood on a dark night, without a light, and find Professor Humboldt's cabin."

"Virginia Wagner evidently did it regularly, Dean."

"Well, she had lots of practice, three years of practice, on bright nights, not-so-bright nights, and dark nights. After doing it enough times, one becomes skilled, doesn't one?"

"I'm sure one does, Dean. The second time for anything is always easier than the first."

"Exactly. So, since you had to get to the cabin before Virginia Wagner, it was necessary that you know the path well. I couldn't believe that you had practiced for this for months and months of dark nights; the only logical conclusion was that you had trod that path yourself many, many times."

"Logical doesn't mean accurate, Dean."

"There are other things that fit, Karen. It was known that Humboldt liked only buxom women. Such as Virginia Wagner. Tinguely is slim and Zapata is downright skinny. But you—those people who think you're Greek because of your husband's name, liken you to the Callipygian Venus."

"My husband likes me the way I am."

"He has good taste. You're a beautiful woman; no one can dispute that. I'm sure Professor Humboldt thought so too. But much as he wanted you, his rigid code would not allow him to dally with a married woman."

"Many men had wanted me; very few had won. I would never be unfaithful to my husband."

"I'm sure. But isn't it odd that with luscious, bereaved Virginia Wagner right in his office, he didn't take her for a full year? Virginia thinks it was because of propriety; he wanted a year to pass after her husband's death, four years ago. I think it was because he preferred you. When did you marry, Karen?"

"Three years ago, as you well know."

"Another peculiar concatenation of events. Humboldt also liked erotic costumes. Do you have any at home?"

"A few. My husband likes them as much as I do."

"A check of the records of the mail order houses might show that your costumes were bought long before you even met your husband."

"Some of my other men friends liked the costumes."

"Did they give you the money to buy them too? I know how little young assistant professors earn."

"It's perfectly fitting for a man to give small gifts to his beloved."

"So it is, Karen. So now we have Professor Humboldt's killer: someone who knew the way to his cabin in the dark, who knew Humbolt's routine and schedule—he was rather rigid in everything he did—who could approach him without his calling the police, who was intelligent enough to invent a new type of crossword puzzle—what did you call it, Karen?"

"'Crossonic' might be a good name."

"An excellent name, Karen. So now we have the constructor of the seventh puzzles—by the way, won't it occur to the police that it was easiest for you to slip that last puzzle into your own attaché case? I guess not; they haven't even made the connection between the Project and the murder yet, and almost three days have passed."

"Is there a connection, Dean? So far you have only very flimsy conjecture."

"True, but there's more. Why go to all the trouble of constructing the puzzles? Couldn't the killer have gone right up to Humboldt and made his demands? Obviously the killer was not only known to Humboldt; he was vulnerable to Humboldt. Humboldt could throw the killer off the Project; he could deny him tenure. He might even use his influence to have him thrown out of the school. So the killer wanted to remain unknown to Humboldt. Sound like anyone you know, Karen?"

"It could be anyone on the Project."

"Not when combined with everything else, Karen, but we'll let that ride for a while. Now, the anonymity was so important to the killer that he was willing to sacrifice his proper share of the proceeds, whatever that was, to remain unknown; was willing to accept one-twelfth rather than, say, the one-half he felt he was entitled to. That means that the total amount of money involved must have been—how much would you say, Karen?"

"As you describe it, Dean, it had to be hundreds of thousands of dollars."

"My thought exactly. Now, how could hundreds of thousands of dollars be involved with the Project, Karen?"

"It couldn't, Dean."

"Not directly, Karen. But peripherally? Suppose that you, Karen, had come up with the idea of the Project. Suppose it was about four years ago, while you were Humboldt's mistress. A lowly assistant professor of English couldn't get very far by herself, but with a mentor as well known and respected as Humboldt, one who controlled a large endowment . . . It was a perfect combination. Of course, the Project was a bit out of Humboldt's line—he's history, not English—but he did have a genuine interest in crosswords, and in making sure people read more, so it required only a little push to . . . What did you wear, Karen? A schoolgirl's uniform? Middy blouse and white socks?"

"That's insulting, Dean." Karen's face shone dark red in the dim light. "I would never *use* sex; you know me better than that."

"I apologize, Karen. Let's say, then, that Humboldt

liked your idea and followed through on it, making you his deputy because you were the best and the brightest. You agreed to take one-twelfth of the income, along with the rest of the group, because there was very little income involved, and because you were sure you would get tenure, recognition, publication of the book, and at least partial credit for this major innovation. The prestige of winning the Liberman Prize was also a consideration, I'm sure."

"If I were in such a position, Dean, don't you think a major part of the motivation would be to help children learn to read, to love reading?"

"Of course, Karen. I'm sure that's what inspired you originally. But then you got married. He seems to be a good man, and you clearly love him. I'm truly happy for you. Unfortunately he's a poet."

"There's nothing wrong with being a poet, Dean. Chris is a very good poet."

"You may be blinded by love, Karen, but even if you're right, there are problems, difficulties. There are very few jobs for poets these days outside of greeting-card companies and advertising agencies. A serious poet needs publication. But the competition is overwhelming. What to do?"

"The university could use a poet in residence, Dean. He might even teach a course or two."

"We can't afford one, Karen; it's much easier to raise money for the football team. The best way for a poet to become known, assuming he's good, is through publication, even in the vanity press. The trouble is that the few thousand dollars per book this requires is not within the reach of an assistant professor, especially if there are two mouths to feed. So where to get the money?"

"Not from the Project, that's for sure."

"No, but one day, in Humboldt's office—you were there regularly, at least three days a week—you noticed a letterhead on Virginia Wagner's desk. Just for a moment, but that was enough. You didn't need to read the letter to know what it meant; the name of the company was enough."

"You credit me with clairvoyance?"

"Not really. Anyone who ever taught knows about— just as I knew what it was before I read the letter. Virginia Wagner, when I interviewed her a second time, mentioned that Humboldt had recently begun dickering with a second publisher. How was that possible? Didn't he already have a contract for the book with the Windham University Press? But when I saw the letterhead, I knew."

"You have the advantage of me, Dean; I never saw any such letterhead. Tell me about it."

"The letterhead—even upside down you could read it easily—said 'Speedy Study Systems, Ltd., of Montana,' the biggest publisher of teaching packets in the country. They put out all those readymade sets of instructional material for teachers, the ones that contain subject matter, lesson plans, spirit masters, transparencies, visual aids, and similar materials for teaching. They're designed for specific grades and levels of proficiency. Many teachers use them."

"Everyone who ever taught is familiar with these packets. Why are you interested in them?"

"Why should Humboldt be corresponding with Speedy? The contract for the book had already been signed. Could he have been thinking of making teaching packets of his lectures on the effects of weapons technology? Not very likely. No, he was going to make a deal with Speedy for the Project, for graded sets of crosswords teaching packets, using Project knowledge and records, the Project techniques, and the by-now-standardized Project puzzles. Full commercialization of the system."

"There are already teaching packets with crosswords in them, Dean."

"Those are not real crosswords, as you know, just one or two words crossing here and there. Dull little things, describing adverbs and adjectives. They don't fool the kids; they're no fun, not what a student would solve for the fun of it. The Project crosswords are *real* crosswords; at each grade level the students would solve them for pleasure. And if you win the Liberman Prize—as you have an excellent chance of doing, from what I hear—

you will be assured of a huge sale of the teaching packets."

"Of course, that was the idea behind the Project: If the student had an incentive to learn, if he *enjoyed* the puzzles, he'd go out of his way to learn. I'm pleased that Professor Humboldt was dealing with Speedy; with your permission we'll continue his negotiations. Maybe we'll produce a generation of readers."

"Also a lot of money, Karen; these sets are expensive. But let's assume no advance at all and, say, a dollar a set royalty. There are forty million students below college age in the country. If only one percent uses the Project crossword sets, that's a royalty of four hundred thousand dollars a year or, if you divide it according to the allocation of the Project's income, one-twelfth to each of you six, thirty-three thousand a year for you. If two percent used these packets, that would make sixty-six thousand per year, and so on. Enough to help your husband become well known, enough so you could take time out to start a family, if that's what you wanted."

"That kind of money would be welcome to me or to any of the others in the Project, assuming we knew about it."

"But you didn't, at least until recently. Humboldt never told you, any of you, about it. Presumably he would have used the money to further some of his other pet projects, and felt that since the idea of commercializing the Project was his, he alone should get all the money. He decided to keep the money, the prestige, the influence on students and teachers, all for himself. He acted as though only the money derived *directly* from the Project was to be shared, as agreed, by the handshake contract. Everything else, including the credit for your idea, would be his. That enraged you. It was not only a betrayal of love, a betrayal of trust, a betrayal of the scholar's ethic; it was depriving your husband of his one chance for recognition. So you decided to get your fair share."

"If this is so, Dean—and it could be so for any of us; we all needed money desperately—why not confront Professor Humboldt directly and demand, say, half the profits rather than be satisfied with one-twelfth?"

"Because of Humboldt's character. You knew that if you approached him directly, he would throw you off the Project, make sure you didn't get tenure, and deny that the Project was your idea. With your word against his, you'd be helpless. There was even the possibility he'd tell your husband about his affair with you, down to the last costume, and claim that you married Chris after Humboldt threw you over. So you decided to play it safe and be satisfied with the one-twelfth. Whatever Humboldt might *suspect*, he could never be *sure* you were the mysterious puzzle constructor."

"There's a hole in your reasoning, Dean. If all this secrecy was necessary, why would the constructor want to meet with Humboldt; to reveal himself and lay himself open to Humboldt's reprisals?"

"When you failed to get Humboldt to share the proceeds properly, you went to him to demand your half share. You figured that with two hundred thousand a year or more, you didn't need tenure or the Project, and that your husband would stick with you—any poet would sell his soul for publication and publicity and, I feel, he really loves you too—with all that money, Chris would not leave you, no matter what Humboldt told him."

"Such a complex negotiation to conclude in five minutes."

"You slipped there, Karen. How would you know the killer had only five minutes?"

"It's logical, Dean. Everyone knew Humboldt kept his door locked. If the killer got there before Virginia Wagner, it could only be because Humboldt left the door unlocked for a few minutes before she came."

"Not necessarily, Karen. He could have let her in himself; I doubt if anyone else but you knew that he made a habit of leaving the door unlocked for his Saturday-night visitors. But we'll let that pass. There was no need for lengthy negotiations. You probably had a paper that said something like this: 'Inasmuch as Mrs. Karen Karas was the originator of the ideas and techniques behind the Crossword Project, I hereby recognize her as co-author of the Project and assign half the proceeds of the proposed sale of the concept and of Project material for commercial and pedagogical use.' Once he signed that, you didn't care what happened to your tenure. But, in fact, it would look very odd if he thereafter opposed your tenure."

"That's very clever, Dean. I wish I had thought of it myself."

Isabel ignored the sarcasm. "However, your desperate gamble failed, as you suspected it might, leaving you open to Humboldt's reprisals, defenseless, without a job, and, maybe, without a husband. So you had to put your alternative plan into action. You killed him."

"Are you saying I brought a gun with me? This jogging suit doesn't even have a pocket."

"Don't play games, Karen; you knew there was a wall full of weapons available. Which weapons, you didn't know, but that wasn't important. You're a big girl, Karen, in good condition, and Humboldt was even smaller than your husband, and considerably older. You maneuvered him into his favorite chair, this one, penned behind his desk, where he liked to be but where he had very little freedom of movement. Then you turned to the wall, one step, picked the nearest weapon, and killed him."

"Just like that? He didn't move, duck, slide to the floor?"

"You knew a teacher's weakness. You took the kukri off the wall, held it horizontally in front of you, right hand, gloved of course, on the hilt, left hand supporting the end of the blade, took one turning step toward Humboldt, and said, 'What is this peculiar-looking sword?' Without thinking, his first reaction would be to say, 'It's a kukri, a Gurkha knife, from India; Nepal, to be exact,' or words to that effect. You lunged forward and stabbed him."

"He didn't move to defend himself?"

"His knowledge prevented that. He knew that a kukri, though it has a sharp point, is not used for stabbing; it's used for chopping, with a downward stroke. Had you lifted it overhead, he might have slid out of the chair or ducked sideways. There would have been plenty of time to do it, although I think you would have gotten him in the end. Besides, he was the epitome of old-fashioned male chauvinism; he couldn't conceive that a woman could attack him with a sword."

"That's an interesting series of guesses, Dean. I'm sure it would make a fascinating whodunit. What does this have to do with me?"

"Still holding out, Karen?"

"There isn't the smallest iota of evidence in what you say. If you took it to the police, they'd throw you out."

"Of course, Karen. That's why I'd like you to confess."

"Whatever for? This is crazy. I didn't kill him."

"I want suspicion removed from your five colleagues, and the matter laid to rest so the damage to Windham is minimized. You can keep your name on the Project and get all the money from the teaching packets. You'll have to leave the school and probably give up teaching, but you'd be rich and your husband will have his chance."

"Much good that will do me in jail."

"You may not go to jail, but if you do, it won't be for very long. Certainly not more than three years. My friend Mr. Sullivan—you met him Sunday—was a famous criminal lawyer. I've learned—I'm sure you can make a deal with the local authorities. You can even claim self-defense, or crime of passion. Or both."

"I have no desire to go to jail, Dean, even for one day. Or even to be known as a killer. Not that I care what others think, but my husband..."

"Karen, you're taking what I say as a suggestion." Isabel's voice grew hard. "It isn't. You're thinking, acting, as though everything I've pointed out is pure guesswork, will not work as proof. You're wrong. This is not an academic exercise, and these are not your fellow professors you're dealing with; the police are practical and sensible. If I tell them what I know, you'll be arrested and indicted."

"They can't arrest anyone without proof, much less indict anyone."

"When they put it all together, Karen, they'll *know* you're the murderer, and they'll make a case against you that will stick. Sure, any one of the items I mentioned is not enough in itself, but all of them put together paint a very clear picture."

"Where's the proof?"

"Are you sure there isn't any, Karen? When you were jogging, you said you waved at people. Did they notice you were wearing gloves on a warm spring night? When you entered the wood, are you sure no one saw you? The police, once they're convinced you're the killer, will question everyone over and over. Someone who did see you, and thought nothing of it, will tell. In the wood itself there are lots of clearings; the kids use them as lovers' lanes. You could pass within six feet of one of them, especially if the pair were lying down, and not see them. Did any of them see you? And when you entered Humboldt's cabin, and when you left, are you positive no one saw you? How about when you left the wood? Are you willing to bet your life on this?"

"You're fishing, Dean. No one saw me, because I wasn't there."

"Are you certain no one knew of your relationship with Humboldt? Virginia Wagner was sure no one knew of hers, but there have been rumors; you must have heard them yourself. When the police start digging, will they turn up someone who saw you entering and leaving Humboldt's cabin every Saturday night? Entering and leaving the woods? A frustrated suitor perhaps?"

"There was no relationship, Dean, so there is nothing to see."

"Over a—what was it, a four-year period? Or more? Five years? Since you were a graduate assistant? Six years? In all these years are you absolutely sure that no one had the slightest inkling that you and Humboldt—? With such regularity? No one wondered why a beautiful young woman like you never was available for a date on Saturday night? No one?"

"Everyone knew that I didn't like to go out with crowds, that I preferred a quiet evening at home."

"But who answered the phone on Saturday night? Did you have a phone phobia that only manifested itself one night a week? And the costumes, Karen, the erotic costumes. How many do you have, Karen? How many did you acquire over a five-year period? One a month? Sixty costumes? That's a lot of money, Karen, for a poor working girl."

"I told you, they were gifts."

"From men friends? How many men friends, Karen? Where are they? Who are they?"

"They must be scattered all over the country by now."

"The police will find them if you give them the names. But so many? How many women in this area, in the whole state, do you think have two closets full of erotic costumes?" Isabel felt a twinge of apprehension here, but went on. "Or are they in your closets? They must be stored somewhere, not in your home. Why? You said your husband likes them; I wonder if he's ever seen more than one. If that many. What would he think if you showed him *all* of them? How would you explain them? Will you tell him what you told me? What you will *have* to tell the police? That men friends gave you the money to buy them? All of them?"

"Chris will stick with me no matter what."

"That may soon be put to the test, Karen, unless you make a deal with the police." Isabel waited. There was no response. "How about the 'Crossonics,' as you call them? Do you have *no* records of them in your apartment? You did no experimenting until you perfected the form? They are a potential source of income; I can't believe you burned all evidence of your invention. What will you tell the police when they find the originals of the three seventh puzzles in your apartment? Under the mattress, or some similar place? They're still there, aren't they? Of course they are; I can tell by your face. You never thought anyone would think of you as the murderer."

"You'd really tell all this garbage to the police, Dean? Knowing what a bastard Fabian Humboldt was?"

"If you go to the police voluntarily, I won't tell anyone anything. You can take all the credit, present the situation as you see fit."

"I'm afraid, Dean, that your promises aren't worth anything. It's clear that you will oppose my tenure no matter what I do, that you will oppose my work on the Project and even the deal with Speedy." Karen took a turning step toward the wall, picked up a short sword with a wavy blade, and stepped back to the front of the desk, holding the hilt in her gloved right hand and the tip of the blade in her left. "What kind of sword is this, Dean?" she asked, and lunged, the point of the sword thrusting toward Isabel's breast.

From the darkness at the far back corner of the room Giles dashed forward, his sword out of the cane, driving toward Karen's heart. As Isabel snapped the big book up from the desk to shield herself, there was a blinding flash of light from the doorway, made all the more blinding by the darkness of the room. Karen stopped dead, dropping the point of her sword, then turned in rage toward the source of the light, lifting the point of the sword again and diving toward the doorway. There was another blinding flash. Karen dropped the sword, put her hands over her eyes, and began crying hysterically.

"It's called a *kris*, Professor Karas," Oliver said.

 38

"**I** HAVE AN EXCELLENT PHOTOGRAPH OF YOU, SIR,"
Oliver said, placing the camera carefully in front of him
on Isabel's table, "about to stab an unsuspecting, unarmed, hysterical woman in the back. Shall I have it en-
larged, sir?"

"I would like those films destroyed, Oliver," Giles said.
"At once."

"I also have a photograph of you, sir, breaking the
police seal and picking the lock. Very slowly, I must say.
Perhaps a practice session might be beneficial, sir?"

"Give me that film," Giles roared.

"But won't it be needed at the trial?" Agatha asked.

"I don't think there will be a trial, Agatha," Giles said.
"Although I can't practice in this state, I spoke informally
to the district attorney. Karen's attorney is very anxious
to make a deal. If the police can put together enough
evidence of the kind Isabel told you about before, her
attorney will agree to almost anything less than premed-
itated murder. If they can't, he'll go for manslaughter.
Don't forget, she still has assault with a deadly weapon,

with intent to kill, hanging over her head. In front of witnesses."

"Captured in Technicolor," Agatha said.

"Yes, well—" Giles got red.

"She tried to kill me, Giles," Isabel said. "You promised to protect me. With your life."

"I knew you were in no danger when I saw you pick up that big book. Karen was not an expert swordsman. My saber would have gotten to her before her kris got to you."

"Would you really have killed a woman, Giles?"

"It would not have been necessary, Isabel. I would have just pinked her. The shock would have caused her to drop her weapon."

"How did you get into the act, Oliver?" Isabel asked.

"When Mr. Giles left his crossword construction notes behind for me to clean up, I inadvertently read the message he intended to transmit. Since we knew who the killer was, it was only necessary for me to prepare for the inevitable. I waited at Professor Humboldt's house, carefully concealed of course, and shortly after Professor Karas entered I went in myself and waited in the dark just outside the study door."

"How did you get there in the first place?" Isabel asked.

"Agatha led me to Professor Humboldt's cottage at two o'clock."

"Why so early? The meeting wasn't until four."

"Professor Karas might have come early, Miss Macintosh, to ambush you and Mr. Giles. If she was carrying a weapon, I wanted to disarm her before you arrived."

"How would you know if she did have a weapon?"

"Amateurs always check their weapons, or at least pat their pockets, when they arrive at the assigned spot."

"But suppose she, too, had decided to come early and waited for us in the cabin?"

"It is most unlikely that she would have broken the police seal. That would have tipped you off and you might not have gone inside. Her purpose, after all, was to find out what you knew."

"And the camera?" Agatha asked.

"Mr. Giles said there was no evidence that would be admissible in court to prove that Professor Karas had committed the murder, so it was obvious that he would try to obtain a confession. That attempt was doomed to failure, of course; Professor Karas is a highly intelligent young woman."

"You deliberately let the murderer who killed Humboldt try to kill me, Oliver?" Isabel was indignant. "I thought you loved me."

"The entire staff has the highest regard for you, Miss Macintosh, but you were never in danger. Professor Humboldt did not expect to be attacked; you did. In fact, you provoked it, if I may say so. I also saw the big thick book on your desk and that your hands grasped it when Professor Karas picked up the kris."

"But a camera, Oliver? Not a gun?"

"Evidence of some crime was needed, Miss Macintosh. I knew that Professor Karas would be in a state of great tension and the flash would not only confuse her; it would blind her sufficiently to enable me to disarm her should it prove necessary. Besides, Mr. Giles was there to distract her."

"Distract?" Giles grew red again. "To *disable* her."

"If you say so, sir," Oliver said calmly.

Agatha quickly changed the subject. "How did you know that sword was a kris, Oliver?"

"One reads a great deal, Agatha. Particularly whodunits."

"I wondered about that, Ollie. When you were out shopping for the camera I cleaned your room. When I moved the suitcases under the bed, they sprang open."

"Sprang open?" Giles was shocked. "Your special suitcases?"

"The locks," Oliver said, "though bulky, are rather old-fashioned, not designed to protect against women who are cleaning."

"Flimsy," Agatha said. "A child could—accidentally... Well, I was flabbergasted to find that they were filled with cleaning equipment and books."

"Books?" Giles said. "Cleaning equipment?"

"Precisely as I described to you, sir," Oliver said. "Communications gear. Devices. Various appointments and contrivances."

"But I thought—"

"Whatever did you bring so many books for, Ollie?"

"It's only Tuesday," Oliver said, "and we're scheduled to stay till Monday morning. I will have lots of time to read."

"I wouldn't count on it, Ollie," Agatha said. "Let's leave Miss Macintosh and Mr. Sullivan alone for a well-deserved rest. You can have your first taste of my special herb tea."

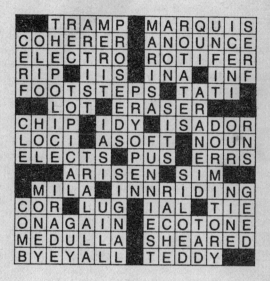

The completed crossword grid reads:

H	A	S	H			P	O	L	E				O	V	O
A	R	T	E			S	O	B	E	R			S	H	E	L
J	E	E	R			T	W	O	O	N	A	H	A	N	D
J	A	M	B	O	R	E	E				M	A	R	I	A
			A	F	A	R			S	E	E	K	E	R	S
S	H	A	R	O	N		M	E	A	D	E				
I	E	R	I			D	M	I	T	R	I		F	L	A
B	R	O	A	D			A	N	I			A	C	R	I	D
S	O	W			A	P	R	O	N	S			H	O	M	E
				K	N	O	T	S			T	R	A	M	P	S
S	P	L	I	C	E	S			S	E	E	N			
I	R	A	T	E					S	C	A	L	D	F	U	R
C	O	N	T	R	A	C	K	E	D			L	I	N	E
K	E	G	S			M	E	A	N	Y			E	N	D	S
O	M	E			P	E	T	E			R	I	O	T

Puzzle No. 3   p. 46

C	R	A	B		A	B	A	S	H		L	A	N	D
I	O	L	E		S	O	R	T	A		A	N	O	A
T	O	O	K		S	P	O	O	L		S	T	U	N
E	M	P	I	R	E		W	R	I	T	H	I	N	G
		L	O	R	D		K	N	O	T				
D	I	C	T	A	T	E	S		G	R	I	N	C	H
E	R	A		M	E	E	T	S		E	M	I	L	Y
B	I	R	D		D	R	E	A	M		E	X	A	M
I	S	L	E	T		E	R	I	E	S		E	R	N
T	H	E	S	I	S		E	L	L	I	P	S	E	S
			O	P	I	E		S	O	L	E			
T	O	O	L	S	E	T	S		D	O	R	E	M	I
E	L	B	A		S	H	O	G	I		I	C	E	S
E	D	I	T		T	E	A	S	E		O	R	L	S
M	E	T	E		A	R	R	A	S		D	U	T	Y

SULLIVAN'S TEST

p. 166

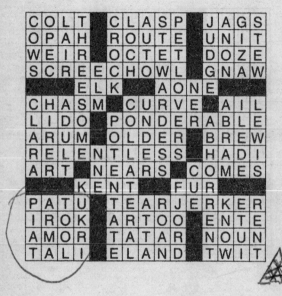

SULLIVAN'S SECOND TEST

p. 172

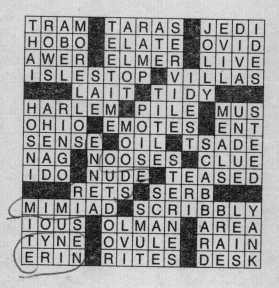

T	R	A	M		T	A	R	A	S		J	E	D	I
H	O	B	O		E	L	A	T	E		O	V	I	D
A	W	E	R		E	L	M	E	R		L	I	V	E
I	S	L	E	S	T	O	P		V	I	L	L	A	S
		L	A	I	T		T	I	D	Y				
H	A	R	L	E	M		P	I	L	E		M	U	S
O	H	I	O		E	M	O	T	E	S		E	N	T
S	E	N	S	E		O	I	L		T	S	A	D	E
N	A	G		N	O	O	S	E	S		C	L	U	E
I	D	O		N	U	D	E		T	E	A	S	E	D
			R	E	T	S		S	E	R	B			
M	I	M	I	A	D		S	C	R	I	B	B	L	Y
I	O	U	S		O	L	M	A	N		A	R	E	A
T	Y	N	E		O	V	U	L	E		R	A	I	N
E	R	I	N		R	I	T	E	S		D	E	S	K

199

From Ballantine

12   TA-43